格雷的老爸

格雷的爷爷

格雷的老妈

格雷的"死党"
——罗利

格雷的弟弟
——曼尼

DIARY
of a Wimpy Kid

小屁孩日记③
——好孩子不撒谎

[美]杰夫·金尼 著

陈万如 译

格雷的哥哥
——罗德里克

格雷

·广州·
广东省出版集团
新世纪出版社

本书简体中文版由美国 Harry N. Abrams 公司通过中国 Creative Excellence Rights Agency 独家授权

版权合同登记号：19-2009-053 号

图书在版编目（CIP）数据

小屁孩日记③：好孩子不撒谎/［美］杰夫·金尼著；陈万如译. —广州：新世纪出版社，2010.1（2010.12 重印）

ISBN 978-7-5405-4218-4

Ⅰ. 小… Ⅱ.①杰… ②陈… Ⅲ. 日记体小说-美国-现代 Ⅳ. J238.2

中国版本图书馆 CIP 数据核字（2009）第 200726 号

出 版 人：陈锐军
选题策划：林 铨 王小斌
责任编辑：王小斌 傅 琨
责任技编：王建慧

小屁孩日记③
——好孩子不撒谎

［美］杰夫·金尼 著 陈万如 译

出版发行：新世纪出版社
经 销：全国新华书店
印 刷：东莞市翔盈印务有限公司
开 本：890mm×1240mm 1/32
印 张：6.75 字 数：135 千字
版 次：2010 年 1 月第 1 版
印 次：2010 年 12 月第 5 次印刷
印 数：65,001－75,000
书 号：ISBN 978-7-5405-4218-4
定 价：14.90 元

质量监督电话：020-83797655 购书咨询电话：020-83793749

有趣的书，好玩的书

夏 致

　　这是一个美国中学男生的日记。他为自己的瘦小个子而苦恼，老是会担心被同班的大块头欺负，会感慨"为什么分班不是按个头分而是按年龄分"。这是他心里一道小小的自卑，可是另一方面呢，他又为自己的脑瓜比别人灵光而沾沾自喜，心里嘲笑同班同学是笨蛋，老想投机取巧偷懒。

　　他在老妈的要求下写日记，幻想着自己成名后拿日记本应付蜂拥而至的记者；

　　他特意在分班时装得不会念书，好让自己被分进基础班，打的主意是"尽可能降低别人对你的期望值，这样即使最后你可能几乎什么都不用干，也总能给他们带来惊喜"；

　　他喜欢玩电子游戏，可是他爸爸常常把他赶出家去，好让他多活动一下。结果他跑到朋友家里去继续打游戏，然后在回家的路上用别人家的喷水器弄湿身子，扮成一身大汗的样子；

　　他眼红自己的好朋友手受伤以后得到女生的百般呵护，就故意用绷带把自己的手掌缠得严严实实的装伤员，没招来女生的关注反惹来自己不想搭理的人；

　　不过，一山还有一山高，格雷再聪明，在家里还是敌不过哥哥罗德里克，还是被耍得团团转；而正在上幼儿园的弟弟曼尼可以"恃小卖小"，无论怎么捣蛋都有爸妈护着，让格雷无可奈何。

　　这个狡黠、机趣、自恋、胆小、爱出风头、喜欢懒散的男孩，一点都不符合人们心目中的那种懂事上进的好孩子形象，奇怪的是这个缺点不少的男孩子让我忍不住喜欢他。

　　人们总想对生活中的一切事情贴上个"好"或"坏"的标签。要是找不出它的实在可见的好处，它就一定是"坏"，是没有价值的。单纯的有趣，让我们增添几分好感和热爱，这难道不是比读书学习考试重要得多的事情吗?! 生活就像一个蜜糖罐子，我们是趴在桌子边踮高脚尖伸出手，眼巴巴地瞅着罐子的孩子。有趣不就是蜂蜜的滋味吗？

　　翻开这本书后，我每次笑声与下一次笑声之间停顿不超过五分钟。一是因为格雷满脑子的鬼主意和诡辩，实在让人忍俊不禁。二是因为我还能毫不费劲地明白他的想法，一下子就捕捉到格雷的逻辑好笑在哪里，然后会心一笑。

　　小学二年级的时候我和同班的男生打架；初一的时候放学后我在黑板上写"某某某（男生）是个大笨蛋"；初二的时候，同桌的男生起立回答老师提问，我偷偷移开他的椅子，让他的屁股结结实实地亲吻了地面……我对初中男生的记忆少得可怜，到了高中，进了一所重点中学，大多数的男生要么是专心学习的乖男孩，要么是个性飞扬的早熟少年。除了愚人节和邻班的同学集体调换教室糊弄老师以外，男生们很少再玩恶作剧了。仿佛大家不约而同都知道，自己已经过了有资格耍小聪明，并且耍完以后别人会觉得自己可爱的年龄了。

如果你是一位超过中学年龄的大朋友，欢迎你和我在阅读时光中做一次短暂的童年之旅；如果你是格雷的同龄人，我真羡慕你们，因为你们读了这本日记之后，还可以在自己的周围发现比格雷的经历更妙趣横生的小故事，让阅读的美好体验延续到生活里。

要是给我一个机会再过一次童年，我一定会睁大自己还没有患上近视的眼睛，仔细发掘身边有趣的小事情，拿起笔记录下来。亲爱的读者，不知道当你读完这本小书后，是否也有同样的感觉？

片刻之后我转念一想，也许从现在开始，还来得及呢。作者创作这本图画日记那年是 30 岁，那么说来我还有 9 年时间呢。

我这么酷的人竟然也被叫成"小·屁孩"，真是@#%&*……

九月

　　我觉得吧，去年要我写日记的决定让老妈很是得意，这不，现在她又买了一个本子给我。记得那时候我怎么说的吗——要是有个呆子看到我揣着一本封面写着"日记"的本子，他们准会闹误会。没错，今天这事的的确确发生了。

（我哥哥罗德里克）

　　既然罗德里克知道我在写第二本日记，我还是记住给它上锁为妙。上几个星期罗德里克拿到我第一本日记，真是一场灾难。你可千万不要勾起我说那个故事呀。

　　即使撇开这个"罗德里克难题"不算，我这个夏天还是过得相当没劲。

　　我们家好玩的地方哪也没去，好玩的事情啥也没做，这都怪老爸。老爸又要我参加游泳队，他要确保今年我一次训练都不落下。

　　老爸深信我命中注定是一位伟大的游泳运动员，于是他每个暑假都要我参加游泳队。

　　几年前我上第一节游泳课的时候，老爸叮嘱我发令枪一响，我就该一头扎进水里往前游。但老爸没有告诉我，发令枪不装子弹，只有弹药没有弹头。

　　比起怎么把自己弄过去泳池的另一端，"子弹到底会落在哪里"这个问题更让我操心。

　　尽管后来老爸跟我解释了"发令枪"是怎么一回事，我仍然是队里游得最慢的人。

　　不过呢，在那个夏末的评奖会上，我得到了"最佳进步奖"，那只是因为与第一次计时赛我的成绩相比，最后一次我快了十分钟。

　　我猜呀，老爸现在依然等着我施展潜力。

啪啪

比起上中学，呆在游泳队更倒霉。这一点有很多事实可以证明。

首先，我们得每天早上7:30到达泳池，那时水总是冷得要命。

其次，我们挤在两条泳道里，跟在我后面的人要越过我的时候，总是会打到我的脚。

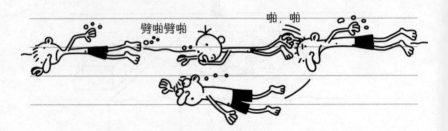

劈啪劈啪　啪，啪

因为水上爵士舞课和游泳训练在同一个时间上课，所以我们只有两条泳道可用。

我确实努力尝试过说服老爸批准我去跳水上爵士舞，别上游泳课，但他就是不买我账。

女士们，加油！
胳膊举高！

4

参加游泳队的第一个夏天，教练叫男孩子穿游泳短裤，别穿那些让身体线条毕露的三角泳裤。但老妈说罗德里克传给我的那条三角裤"好得很"。

游泳训练结束后，罗德里克会开着乐队训练用的小·货车来接我回家。老妈突发奇想：要是格雷和罗德里克每天能在车上度过一段"黄金时光"，他们就不会老打架。事实证明老妈这样做只会雪上加霜。

罗德里克接我总是晚到半小·时，而且他不让我坐在前座。他说泳池水中的氯会弄坏坐垫，全然不顾小·货车已经上了十五岁的事实。

罗德里克的车后厢压根没有座位，我只好蜷缩在一堆乐器中间。每次车一停，我就得祷告一番：罗德里克的鼓千万别把我的头砸离脖子呀。

最后，我还是选择每天自个儿走路回家，不蹭罗德里克的车。再怎么说，走两里路总比在车后厢砸个脑震荡要强吧。

① 见《小屁孩日记①》。

夏天才过了一半，我已经在游泳队受够了。我想了一个小伎俩来逃课。我先下水游几圈，一会儿就跟教练申请上洗手间。之后我就躲在那里，等训练结束了才出来。我的计划只有一个美中不足的地方：男厕所的温度只有40华氏度①，呆在那里比在泳池里冷得多。

我只好用卫生纸把自己裹起来，免得患上低体温症。

这个夏天我一大块时间就是这么过的。现在你知道我为什么会盼着明天学校开学了吧。

---

① 约等于4.4摄氏度。

星期二

今天我回到学校，周围每个人对我都怪怪的。刚开始我还没意识到发生了什么。

没多久我记起来了：我身上还附着去年的"千年奶酪"。上学期最后一个星期我惹上它，过了暑假回来我忘得一干二净了。

"奶酪附体"的麻烦之处，是你得把它传给下一个人，自己才能脱身。但没人敢走进我周围三十英尺范围内，我就知道这个学年都会给"奶酪附体"断送了。

走运的是，班上新来了一个叫杰瑞米·平道尔的小孩，这个问题一下子就解决了。

第一节课上初等代数，老师让我坐在亚历克斯·阿鲁达旁边，他是班上最聪明的学生。

抄亚历克斯的卷子超级容易，因为他每次都早早做完，并把试卷搁在他身旁的地面上。每次到了危急关头，我就知道可以指望亚历克斯来搭救我，这种感觉真不错。

那些姓氏首字母是字母表头几个字母的小·孩，经常会在课堂上被老师点名回答问题，所以他们最后都成为学习高手。

有些人不信真有此事。要是你来参观我的学校，我可以证明给你看。

亚历克斯·阿鲁达

克里斯托弗·泽格尔

突破这个"姓氏规则"的小·孩我只想到一个——彼得·尤特格。上五年级之前，彼得一直是班上成绩最好的小孩。

五年级的时候，每当有人喊他名字，我们一群小·孩就拿他名字的首字母来开玩笑，搞到他的日子很不好过。

① 彼得·尤特格的姓名首字母缩写是PU，读音跟俚语pee-you一样，嗅到难闻的味道时人们说pee-you表示状恶，另外把长U的发音，PU的读音便跟俚语pooh（粪便）一样，格雷以此来笑话彼得。

现在，彼得不怎么举手发言了，他的成绩平平无奇。

"臭臭"的事情和彼得的变化让我心中有点不安。可要我放弃一个可以自吹自擂的机会，真是太难啊！

不管怎么说，今天每节课我的座位都挺不错，第七节的历史课除外。这节课教我们的是霍夫老师，有件事情让我知道几年前他教过罗德里克。

　　老妈一直要我和罗德里克分担更多家务活。现在我们俩每晚负责洗碗。老妈规定，不洗干净碗碟，我们就别想看电视打游戏。可是我想在这里说一句，罗德里克是这个世界上最恶劣的洗碗搭档。

　　一吃完晚饭，他就上楼到洗手间扎营，一呆就是一小时。等他下楼回到厨房时，我早完工了。

　　每次我向老爸老妈投诉他的劣迹时，罗德里克总会拿出同一个馊理由：

老爸老妈太操心我的小·弟弟曼尼了，哪里顾得上我和罗德里克的战争。

　　昨天老爸老妈在曼尼书包里翻出来一张画，那是曼尼在幼儿园画的。这张画让他们十分伤心。老爸老妈都以为画的是他们，他们在曼尼面前表现得无比恩爱。

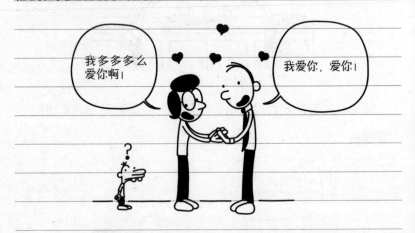

　　可是我知道曼尼真正要画的人是谁：我和罗德里克。
　　前一天晚上我和罗德里克为了抢电视遥控器狠狠打了一架，曼尼目睹了整个战况。不过这些老爸老妈不需要知道。

　　夏天过得糟糕的另一个原因在于我最好的朋友——罗利。他几乎整个假期都在旅游。我印象中他是去了南美还是哪里，但到底是哪里，老实说，我真的不大清楚。

　　要我对别人的旅程感兴趣，真的挺难。我不知道自己这样子算不算是坏孩子。

　　还有一点，罗利一家好像总在准备着到世界上哪个稀奇古怪的地方旅游，我永远也搞不懂他们去那些地方干吗。

　　另一个让我不在意罗利到哪旅行的原因是，不论何时罗利出游回来，他都会逼我听他喋喋不休。

　　去年罗利一家去了澳大利亚十天，不过你从他回来那天的举动来看，你会以为他在那里呆了一辈子。

13

　　另一件事也很烦人，罗利每到一个新地方，不管那里正在流行什么，他都会趋之若鹜。

　　比如说，两年前罗利从欧洲回来，迷上了一个叫"约希"的流行歌手。我还以为那是一个大明星。罗利回来时，包里全是那家伙的唱片和海报。

　　我瞅了罗利的唱片一眼，跟他说约希的歌是给六岁的小·姑娘

① 这里罗利用澳大利亚英语跟格雷打招呼，原文是"G'day, mate！"

听的，他不信我。罗利反驳说我不过是妒忌他"发现"了约希。

那时候这家伙成了罗利的新偶像，真恼人。我说的批评约希的话，罗利都当耳边风。

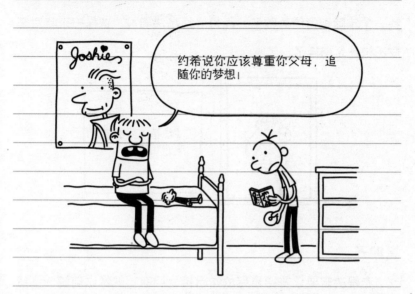

约希说你应该尊重你父母，追随你的梦想！

说到外国，今天上法语课，勒弗雷尔太太说今年我们要选择笔友。

罗德里克上初中的时候，他的笔友是一个十七岁的荷兰女孩。我知道这一点是因为我在他的垃圾抽屉里看到女孩的信。

我喜欢阳光灿烂的日子，喜欢吃冰淇淋。你喜欢吗？

勒弗莱太太发放表格时，我仔仔细细检查了每一格内容，这样做是为了像罗德里克一样找到那样一个漂亮笔友。

　　但勒弗莱太太看完我的表格后，叫我重新填一张。她说我要找一个年龄相仿的男孩子，而且必须是法国人。这样一来我对笔友不抱什么期待了。

（法语）我的名字叫菲利普。

星期五

　　老妈决定要让罗德里克放学后接我回家，就像以前游泳训练后他来接我一样。我想她并没有从上次的经验中吸取教训。但我有。所以今天罗德里克来接我的时候，我拜托他刹车别那么急。

　　罗德里克说没问题，接着他故意绕路，不放过镇上任何一个减速带。

我下车时，冲罗德里克大喊"大混蛋"，接着我们打了起来。老妈在客厅里透过窗户看得一清二楚。

老妈叫我们进去，坐在餐桌边上。她说我和罗德里克要使用"文明的方式"来解决我们的纷争。

老妈对我和罗德里克说，我们要写检讨，写明自己做错了什么，并且配上一张图。我知道老妈从哪里学来这一招。

老妈以前是个学前班老师，每当班上有小孩做错事，她就会让他画一张画。我猜这样做的目的是让那个小孩为自己的行为感到羞愧，以后再也不犯同样的错。

这样说吧，老妈这招在四岁小孩身上也许很管用，但她要想我和罗德里克和平共处，还得另想他法。

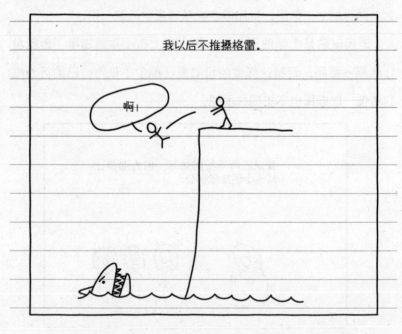

事情的真相是，罗德里克能够对我为所欲为，因为他知道我拿他一点办法也没有。

看，罗德里克是唯一一个知道我暑假那桩大糗事的人，从那时起他一直拿这要挟我。要是我告发他的任何一件坏事，他就会向全世界宣扬我的秘密。

我多希望我也抓到他的把柄，和他扯平。

罗德里克有一件糗事是给我知道了，但我觉得从这件事上占不了什么便宜。罗德里克上高二那年，拍年度手册照片的前一天他病倒了，老妈让老爸把罗德里克高一拍的照片寄到学校。老爸把罗德里克小学二年级的照片寄过去。别问我老爸怎么会犯这样的糊涂。

信不信由你，学校居然把那张照片照印不误。

李奥纳多·哈里顿　安德鲁·哈特利　罗德里克·赫夫利　　海瑟·希尔

可惜的是，罗德里克还不笨，撕掉了年度手册的那一页。如果我要找点东西对付他，还得努力发掘。

自从老妈派了洗碗的任务给我和罗德里克，老爸丢下饭碗就到地下室，打造他的"美国内战战场微缩模型"。

老爸每晚至少在那里呆三个小时。如果可以，老爸会很乐意整个周末都围着模型转。不过老妈对他另有安排。

老妈喜欢租碟看爱情喜剧，要老爸陪她看，但我知道老爸只是在等机会脱身回到地下室。

亲吻
拥吻

20

要是老爸不能下去地下室，他就会用尽办法使孩子们和地下室保持距离。

　　老爸不会让我或者罗德里克靠近他的战场模型，他觉得我们一定会砸了它。

　　今天早些时候，我无意中听到老爸跟曼尼说话，告诫他不要在那里摸来摸去。

刚才我听到地下室里传出"呼噜呼噜"的声音。

星期六

　　罗利今天来我家。老爸不喜欢罗利来，他说罗利"容易出事"。我觉得嘛，那是因为有一次罗利在我家吃晚饭，不小心把碟子掉地上摔碎了。

　　所以现在老爸认定，罗利一个笨手笨脚的动作就会摧毁他整个内战战场。

这些天不管罗利什么时候来我家，他收到的第一句问候语是：

罗利爸爸也不喜欢我。所以我不怎么去他家了。

我在罗利家的最后一夜，我们一起看了一部电影。电影里面一群小孩发明了自己的密语，没一个大人听得懂。

一到2:30，我们一起把课本扔到地板上。

我和罗利都觉得那样子很酷，就试着破解电影里面小·孩子说的语言。

但我们一点也搞不懂，于是我们自创了一套密语。

我们在晚餐时试验了一下我们的密语。

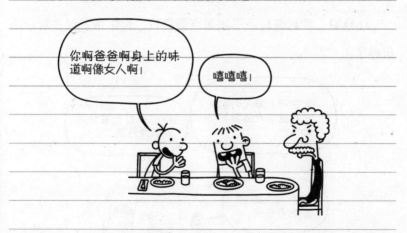

但罗利老爸一定是破解了我们的密码，因为我还没吃甜品就被撵回家。从那以后我再也没收到过去罗利家过夜的邀请。

　　罗利今天带了一叠他去旅游的照片过来。他说最棒的一段旅程是他们在河上漂流，还给我看那些拍得模模糊糊的小鸟照片。

　　跟你说，我去过野外王国游乐场很多回了，那里也有这个河道漂流的玩意，河上还有黑猩猩和恐龙之类的机器动物，太好玩了。

　　让我说，罗利爸妈还不如省点冤枉钱，直接带罗利去游乐场玩好了。

当然啦，罗利对我的故事没兴趣，他收起照片，回家去。

今天晚饭后，老妈要老爸看她租的电影碟，可老爸真的很惦念他的内战战场。趁老妈中途上洗手间，老爸在被子里塞了好几个枕头，看起来就像是他在睡觉。电影播完后，老妈才发现老爸已经金蝉脱壳。尽管那时只是晚上8:30，她还是到地下室把老爸赶上床。

曼尼现在和老爸老妈一起睡，他害怕住在地下室的怪兽。

星期二

我以为我已经听完了罗利的旅行故事，我错了。昨天我们的社会研究课老师叫罗利给全班介绍他的旅行。今天他就穿着一套滑稽的衣服来上学。更糟糕的是几个女孩吃午饭时跟罗利搭讪，还拍他马屁。

不过没过多久我就意识到这也不是一件坏事。我带着罗利在饭堂里四处招摇，不管怎么说，他是我最铁的哥们嘛。

星期六

过去几个星期六，老爸都带我去购物中心。刚开始我以为他想多点时间陪我，不过后来我明白了，他是为了避开罗德里克的乐队排练。这一点我完全能理解他。

罗德里克和他的重金属乐队每到周末就在地下室排练。

乐队的主唱是一个叫比尔·瓦尔特的家伙，今天我和老爸从家里走出来的时候遇见了他。

赫夫利先生早上好！

比尔没有工作，他还在和父母一起住，尽管他已经35岁了。

我很肯定老爸最怕的就是罗德里克会把比尔当成偶像，以后有样学样。

所以老爸每次见到比尔，接下来一整天的心情都好不到哪里去。

罗德里克邀请比尔参加他的乐队，理由只有一个：比尔当选过"最有希望成为摇滚明星的人"，那是在比尔上高中的时候。

最有希望成为摇滚明星的人

比尔·瓦尔特　　　安娜·伦瑟姆

　　到现在为止，"摇滚明星"的奖项在比尔身上还没有兑现。我记得我听说安娜·伦瑟姆如今呆在牢房里。

　　不管怎么说，我和老爸今天在购物中心逛了好几个小时，可我们回到家时，罗德里克和乐队还在排练。一个街区以外的地方你都可以听到吉他声和鼓声。一群游手好闲的小年轻在我家门外的路上晃荡。

　　他们一定是听到地下室传出的音乐声，被吸引住了，这情形有点像飞蛾被灯光吸引住了。

　　老爸看到那些路上的小年轻，简直要疯掉了。

老爸跑进屋里要打电话叫警察来，在他按下911之前老妈拦住了他。

老妈说那些小年轻又没干什么坏事，只不过"欣赏"罗德里克的音乐而已。我都不知道她怎么能一脸正经地说出这些话。要是你听过罗德里克的乐队表演，你就知道我说的是什么意思。

只要那些小年轻还在，老爸就安不了心。

于是老爸上楼拿他的音响下来，放进一张古典音乐的唱片，音乐响起来了。那些小年轻消失得有多快，说你都不信。

老爸为自己想出这样的绝招洋洋自得，可老妈控告他故意赶走罗德里克的"乐迷"。

星期天

　　今天我妈开车载我和曼尼上教堂，路上我对曼尼挤眉弄眼，努力逗他笑。有一个鬼脸让曼尼笑疯了，苹果汁从他鼻子里喷出来。

可老妈发话了：

好吧，一旦老妈把这个想法放进曼尼的脑袋里，一切都完了。

　　看到没？这就是我始终跟曼尼保持距离的原因。每次我想逗他一下，结果都让我后悔不已。我还记得我小一点的时候，听到老妈老爸跟我说我很快会有一个小弟弟，心里不知有多高兴。

　　被罗德里克欺负了那么多年，我当然十分乐意升上大哥的位置。

可老妈老爸总是对曼尼呵护备至，我想碰他一根指头都不行，哪怕是曼尼罪有应得的时候。

拿前几天的事情来说，我的电子游戏机插上电源不能启动。我拆开一看，原来曼尼把巧克力曲奇饼塞进了碟仓里。

曼尼每次破坏我的东西，总是用同一个借口，这次当然不例外。

我真想好好教训曼尼一顿，但老妈站在我旁边，我啥也做不了。

老妈说她会和曼尼"好好谈一下"，然后他们就下楼了。半小·时后，他们回到我的房间里，曼尼手里捧着一坨东西。

那是一坨插满牙签的锡纸，牙签尖尖的一端露在外头。

不要问我这坨玩意怎么补偿我受损的电子游戏机。我准备扔了这坨蠢物，可老妈不让我这么做。

我得逮个机会把它扔进垃圾箱。记住我的话，要是我不让它消失，最后我会一屁股坐在上面。

　　尽管曼尼让我气结，有他在身边还是有个好处。自从曼尼会说话，罗德里克就不再逼我为他学校的筹款活动卖巧克力条。这回你相信我，我很感激他的决定。

星期一

勒弗雷尔太太今天让我们写第一封给笔友的信。她指定了一个叫马马杜的小·孩做我的笔友，我想他住在法国某个地方。

我知道我应该写法语，而马马杜应该写英语，不过说老实话，用外语写信真的很难。我看不出我们俩有什么必要为笔友通信弄得筋疲力尽。

> 亲爱的马马杜，
>
> 　首先，我认为我们俩都应该写英语，那样多
>
> 简单。

还有一件事，记得我说过我最后会坐在曼尼那坨刺人的锡纸团上吗？我说对了一半。

罗利今天来我家打游戏，坐到锡纸团上面的人是他。

其实说老实话，我松了一口气。几天前我就找不着那坨东西了，我很庆幸最后它以这样的结果露面了。

35

在混乱中，我把曼尼的"礼物"甩进垃圾箱。我知道老妈这回不会阻止我。

<u>星期三</u>

罗德里克明天得交一篇英语论文，老妈让他这回自己做。罗德里克不会打字，通常他在笔记本上手写，然后交给老爸打字。

老爸读了罗德里克的论文，发现各种各样的事实错误。

罗德里克才不在乎那些错误，他叫老爸不用管那么多，按照他写的打字就是。

可老爸受不了打一份错漏百出的论文，所以他把罗德里克的论文重写了一遍。几天之后，罗德里克得意地拿着他的满分论文回家，那样子就像论文是他自己写的一样。

就这样过了好几年，我觉得老妈已经下定决心要改变这种状况。所以今晚她告诫老爸，罗德里克这次要自己做作业，禁止老爸帮他忙。

罗德里克吃过晚饭就进了电脑房，你可以听得出他大概一分钟打一个字母。

我敢说，罗德里克打字的声音烦死老爸了。最烦人的是，罗德里克每十分钟就从电脑房出来，问老爸一个愚蠢的问题。

空格键又在哪里呀？

这样过了几个小时，老爸终于受不了了。

老爸等老妈睡了，就帮罗德里克敲完整篇论文。看来罗德里克还是可以靠老爸罩着，至少这一次是这样。

敲
敲
敲

我明天要交一份读书报告，不过我不打算卖力干活。很久之前我就发现了做读书报告的秘诀。过去五年我一直用同一本书来混分数：《夏洛克·萨米又破案了》。

　　《夏洛克·萨米又破案了》这本书有大约20个短篇小说，我把每篇小说都当成一本书，老师从来没发现。这些故事大同小异。无非是有个大人犯罪了，然后夏洛克·萨米发现了真相，让那个人出丑。

　　现在我已经成了一个写读书报告的半吊子专家。你要做的全部事情，就是写下老师爱听的话，这就够了。

38

十月

<u>星期一</u>

  去年我有一个叫齐拉格·古普塔的朋友，今年六月他搬家到外地。当时他们一家开了一个盛大的告别派对，所有的邻居都参加了。不过我觉得齐拉格的家人一定是改变了主意，因为今天齐拉格回到学校来。

  大家看到齐拉格回来都很高兴。我们几个人决定在正式欢迎他回来之前逗他一下。

  我们假装他还没回来。

  我得承认，这样很好玩。

　　午饭的时候，齐拉格坐在我旁边。我的便当多了一块巧克力曲奇，我充分发挥了它的作用。

好吧，这一回我有点残忍。

狼吞虎咽咔哧咔哧

我想我们可能明天就放过齐拉格。继上一次"臭臭"事件之后，这一次"隐形齐拉格"又会是我大放异彩的机会。

星期二

好吧，"隐形齐拉格"的玩笑还在继续，全班都在耍他。我不想太早下结论，不过呢，我觉得自己真的可能会因为想出这个点子而得到"班级活宝"的称号。

上科学课时，老师叫我数一下教室里有多少人，好让她知道该从柜子里拿出多少副护目镜。

我当众上演了一场大戏，每个人我都数了，就是不数齐拉格。

33……34！这节课有34人。

当然，这回齐拉格忍不住了。他站起来大声叫嚷，这个时候要眼睛直视前方当他不存在，真的很困难。

我想告诉他我们从来没有说过他不是个人，只不过他是一个"隐形"人。但我还是管住了自己的嘴巴。

在你合上本子并说我捉弄齐拉格真是个损友时，请允许我替自己辩护：我的个子比我们学校95%的小孩矮，所以要找一个可以被我戏弄的人，我的选择范围很有限。

而且，想出这主意也不能全怪我。你信不信都好，我是从老妈那里学来这一招的。当我还很小的时候，有一次我在餐桌底玩，老妈到处找我。

我不知道当时我为什么那样做，但我还是决定要和老妈开个玩笑，躲在那里不出来。

　　老妈喊着我的名字走遍整个房子。我想最后她一定发现了我躲在餐桌下，但她仍然假装不知道我在哪。

　　那时我觉得真好玩，我还准备在那里多呆一会儿。最后老妈来了一招杀手锏，她自言自语说要把我的糖果机送给罗德里克。

　　所以呢，要是你要批评我发明了"隐形齐拉格"，现在你该知道要怪谁了吧。

　　好啦，昨天齐拉格已经放弃了让我们班上的人跟他说话的努力。不过今天他发现了我们的死穴。

　　我都忘了罗利。这个玩笑刚诞生的时候，我就让罗利远离齐拉格，因为我预感到罗利会穿帮。

　　不过我还是太自信了，放松了警惕。

　　齐拉格午饭时就在罗利身上下功夫，他差点就得逞了。

我看得出罗利很快就会投降，得迅速行动。我跟在场的人说，一根玉米热狗肠正漂浮在餐桌上方，我把它拽下来，咬成两段。

　　多亏我反应够敏捷，这个玩笑才没有穿帮。

　　这下齐拉格恼了。他掐我手臂，当然喽，我得装着没感觉。

　　跟你说，这真的不好装。虽然齐拉格个子小，但他掐人非常在行。

星期五

准是齐拉格向不知哪个老师告我的状，因为今天我被叫去行政办公室。

我到了副校长罗伊的房间，他一脸怒气。他知道了我发起这个恶作剧的过程，对我发表了一场关于"尊重"和"正当"之类的演讲。

幸运的是，有一个关键的事实罗伊校长弄错了，那就是被我们捉弄的受害者。这样一来，道歉就容易多了。

看起来罗伊校长对我的道歉相当满意，没有罚我放学后留堂就放我走了。

以前我总是听别人说，每回训完一个学生，罗伊校长都会给他一颗棒棒糖，拍着他的背送他出去。我的亲身经历可以向你证明那是真的。

舔

星期六

明天是罗利的生日派对，老妈带我去购物中心买礼物送给他。我选了一个刚面世的电子游戏，递给老妈让她付钱。可她说我得用自己的钱买。

我跟她说，首先，我一穷二白。

其次，即便我有钱，我也不会浪费在罗利身上。

听了我的话老妈不大高兴，可财政破产不是我的错呀。暑假我找了一份工作，可我的雇主骗了我的劳动力，我一文钱也没挣到。

和我们家隔了几户的邻居，男主人姓福勒。每个夏天他们一家人都出外度假。他们养了一条叫王子的狗，通常他们外出前都把狗寄养了，不过今年他们跟我说，愿意每天付我五美元，条件是我每天喂狗，带它散步。我算了一下，一个夏天下来这笔钱够我买一堆电子游戏了。

　　王子可能太害怕在陌生人面前拉便便，结果我每天都得在大太阳下面站好长时间，等这只笨狗拉完才能走。

快点啦！

　　我等来等去，它一动不动，于是我干脆带它回屋里。

　　可我每次一走，王子就在房子的前厅拉便便，弄得一塌糊涂，第二天我得去清理干净。到了暑假末，我突然醒悟，与其天天干活，不如到了最后那天一次性把王子的便便清理干净，多省事。

　　接下来的两周，我只管喂王子，任它在前厅地板上干它想干的事。

福勒夫妇按计划回来前的一天，我带齐清洁工具到福勒家。

但你猜怎么着？福勒夫妇缩短了行程，提前一天回来了。他们大概不知道自己改变计划之后，礼貌的做法是应该提前通知别人一声。

今天晚上老妈召集我和罗德里克开家庭会议。她说我们两个总是抱怨没钱，她想到一个让我们赚钱的办法。

说着她掏出一叠桌面游戏的道具钞票，美其名曰"母元"。老妈说我们每次做了家务或者别的好事，我们就能挣到母元。母元可以兑成真钱。

　　老妈给了我们每人1000母元做启动资金。1000元哪！我以为自己马上可以富起来了，可她接着解释说，一母元只能换真的一分钱。

　　老妈告诉我们如何积攒母元，要是我们的耐心足够，就可以买到自己想要的东西。

　　老妈还没说完，罗德里克就向老妈提出用他手上的全部母元立即兑换真钱，然后他好下楼去便利店，把钱贡献给摇滚杂志。

　　罗德里克喜欢怎么样浪费自己的钱都行，我可要精打细算。

星期天

　　今天罗利开生日派对，地点是购物中心。要是我只有七岁，我肯定会觉得派对很好玩。

　　七岁是参加派对的小·孩的平均年龄。罗利邀请了整个空手道队的人，他们大部分还是小·学生。我要是早点知道派对的安排，那我就不来了。

　　一开始我们玩"贴驴子尾巴"那些无聊游戏。最后一个游戏是躲猫猫。我本来打算躲在波波池里，等派对结束了再出来。不过那里已经有一个小·孩了。这个小·孩不是参加罗利派对的。他参加的是一个小·时前的另一场派对。

　　我想他也是在那里玩躲猫猫，好让人找不到他。

　　因为工作人员必须给这个小·孩找爸妈，罗利的派对不得不暂停。

　　之后情况就好起来了。我们吃了蛋糕，围观罗利拆礼物。大部分都是小屁孩才玩的玩具，可罗利似乎很喜欢自己的礼物。

　　猜猜罗利爸妈送他什么礼物？一本日记本。

　　我有点不爽，因为我知道罗利为了仿效我才问他爸妈要日记本。罗利打开礼物后说：

我撞了他胳膊一下，好让他清楚地知道我。我才不管他生日不生日。

有一件事我得声明。以前我觉得老妈买给我的日记本太女孩子气了，心里老大不乐意。不过看到罗利的日记本，我就再不觉得有什么了。

最近罗利模仿我做的一切。他看我看的漫画书，喝我喝的汽水。老妈说我应该觉得"很有面子"，可老实说，我心里发毛。

几天前，我想看看罗利能学我学到什么地步，于是我做了一个试验。

我卷起一只裤腿，在另一只脚踝上系上一条艳丽的方巾。这就是我今天上学的装束。

果然不出我所料，第二天罗利上学，跟我的打扮一模一样。

所以我这个星期再度造访了罗伊副校长的办公室。

有几个混混在我家房子外面显摆他们帮派的标志。

星期一

我以为"隐形齐拉格"这件事已经和我撇清干系了，没想到我错了。

今天晚上老妈接到齐拉格爸爸的电话。古普塔先生一五一十地跟我妈说我们要他儿子的事，我是罪魁祸首。

老妈马上来质问我，我说我压根就不知道齐拉格爸爸说的事。

然后老妈拉着我去罗利家，听他怎么说。

还好，我一早就预备了会有这样一天的。我已经反复训练过他，如果我们被突击审讯，只要我们俩都矢口否认，那就没事。

但老妈一开口问罗利，他就崩溃了。

去完罗利家，老妈赶着我去齐拉格家道歉。跟你说，这一点都不好玩。

　　古普塔先生似乎对我的道歉不大满意。信不信由你，齐拉格居然很受用。

　　我道歉后，齐拉格邀我进屋里打电子游戏。我猜呀，齐拉格终于找到同学跟他说话，一颗悬着的心总算放了下来，所以他彻底原谅了我这个始作俑者。

　　于是我也原谅了他。

星期二

　　虽然齐拉格昨晚放过了我，但老妈还没饶我。

　　其实她生气的原因不是我发起这个玩笑或者捉弄齐拉格。她恼的是我撒谎。

老妈警告我，要是她再发现我撒谎，她就关我一个月的禁闭，不让我打游戏。

这个时候我最好夹紧尾巴做人，老妈从不会忘记自己说过的话。我做过的坏事她记得一清二楚。

你是第二次把鞋底的泥带到厨房里了！

（第一次：六年前）

去年有一回老妈逮住我扯谎，我为此付出了惨痛代价。

那是圣诞节前一星期，老妈做了一个姜饼小房子，放在冰箱顶上面。她下令说圣诞夜之前谁都不许碰它。

可我控制不住自己。每天晚上，我偷偷下楼，从姜饼房子上掰下一小块。我忍着馋每次只吃一点点，那样老妈就不会觉察到姜饼有什么变化。

可是，要限制自己每次只吃像水果糖或者面包屑那样的一点点姜饼，真是难啊。但我总算熬过来了。

我都不知道自己究竟吃了多少。当圣诞夜老妈从冰箱顶把姜饼拿下来的时候，我知道了。

老妈拿我是问，我抵赖说上面的糖果不是我吃的。我真希望自己当时就老实交代，这个小谎把我害惨了。

老妈刚接受了给一家本地报纸育儿专栏撰稿的工作，她整天到处找素材。这下好了，我成了本地名人。

当你的孩子撒谎

苏珊·赫夫利

圣诞节的前一个星期会给孩子带来压力，这段期间会对他们产生难以预想的诱惑力。我的儿子格雷……

我现在回想起来，觉得老妈在诚信方面也不是无懈可击。

记得在我还小的时候，老妈发现我没有每晚刷牙，就假装给牙医打电话。我现在一天刷牙四次，就是那个电话的作用。

卡拉茨医生，你有没有给小男孩用的假牙？只有木头做的假牙？那也行。

星期五

好啦，三天过去了，我遵守了对老妈的承诺。现在我时时刻刻百分百诚实。信不信由你，这没多大难度。

59

事实上，我还得到解放呢。在几个场合我都比前一个星期要诚实得多。

比如说，前几天我和邻家一个叫肖恩·斯奈拉的小·孩聊天。

等我长大了，我要做一名专业的篮球运动员。

肖恩你还是三思吧！你和你爸妈的身高都不足五尺二寸（约1.57米），在我认识的人当中只有你六岁就重200磅！

呜哇哇！

我不能撒谎.

昨天，罗利一家给他爷爷举行生日派对。

　　大多数的人似乎都不欣赏像我那么诚实的人。所以别问我乔治·华盛顿是怎么当上总统的。

星期六

　　今天家长教师协会的基尔曼太太打电话来找老妈，我接了电话，准备叫老妈来听，但她低声示意我对基尔曼太太说她不在家。

我分不清老妈是不是在引诱我撒谎或者犯什么禁，不过我可不会在这么愚蠢的事情上毁掉我诚实的清誉。

于是我让老妈出去门外的走廊后，才跟基尔曼太太说话。

我妈妈现在不在屋里。

从老妈进屋后的神情，我已经感觉到她不会再管我那个"诚实的承诺"了。

星期一

今天是学校的职业发展日。学校设立这么一个日子是为了引导我们规划未来的人生。

他们请了一群来自不同行业的大人。他们以为这样子我们就会发现自己喜欢什么工作，继而知道自己长大后想做什么。

事实上是你只会发现有什么工作自己绝对不做。

介绍会之后，我们要填写一份问卷。第一个问题是：十五年后你会在哪里？

我清清楚楚地知道十五年后我会在哪里：在我的别墅里，在游泳池边上，数着我的钱。可问卷没有这一个选项。

人们希望问卷的结果能够预测你长大后会从事什么工作。我

填完后看了结果，我的工作是"小·职员"。

他们制作这份问卷时一定有些地方弄错了，我可没听说过有哪个小·职员是亿万富翁。

其他小·孩也对测试结果不满意。不过老师说我们对此不用太认真。

谁信老师这些鬼话。就拿爱德华·米利来说吧，去年他的测试结果是"卫生清洁工"，自此以后老师们都对他另眼相看。

罗利的测试结果是"护士"，这个结果似乎令他很高兴。有几个女孩的测试结果也是护士，下课后她们都跟罗利说话。

明年我得记住坐在罗利旁边，抄他的问卷，享受一下女生找我说话的待遇。

星期六

我和罗德里克今天在家里闲着没事，老妈让我们去奶奶家帮忙耙落叶。老妈说我们清理一袋落叶她就给100母元。另外，奶奶答应清理干净后给我们喝热巧克力。

我真不想在星期六工作，可我需要钱。而且奶奶做的热巧克力特别好喝。我们从家里的车库拿了几个耙和塑料袋，就直奔奶奶家。

我和罗德里克各扫院子的一边。干了十分钟，罗德里克过来说我全做错了。

罗德里克说我每袋装的叶子太多，如果我扎袋子的位置低一些，我就可以装多一些袋子。

看，这就是你会从大哥那里得到的忠告。

罗德里克告诉我这个偷懒的办法后，我们装袋子的速度就奇快无比，半小·时就把带去的全部袋子装完了。

我们进屋里时，奶奶似乎不大乐意拿出热巧克力来。大人也真是的，说话不算数！

星期一

　　打"职业发展日"那天起，罗利就天天和几个女孩坐在餐厅角落的桌子共进午饭。他们一群人简直就像是"美国未来的护士联盟"。

　　别问我他们到底在那里谈些啥。他们只是低声交谈，像小学一年级的孩子那样"哧哧"地笑。

　　我可以说的是，他们最好不是在谈论我。

　　你还记得我说过吗？知道我暑假发生的糗事的人，只有罗德里克一个。我可以说，罗利知道我第二糗的事，我真不希望他把事情翻出来。

　　上五年级的时候，我们上了一个西班牙语的课程，要在全班面前表演一个滑稽短剧。我的拍档是罗利。

　　整个短剧都要用西班牙语表演。罗利问要是给我一根巧克力糖，我愿意表演什么。我说我会倒立。

　　可是，当我脚上头下的时候，我滑下来了，屁股擦着墙壁往右滑下来。

埃斯塔里奥一动不动地附在我身上啊啊啊!

　　学校从不为修补墙壁的事操心。在小学余下的时光，我的屁股印一直展览在冈萨雷斯太太的教室。

　　要是罗利把这个故事宣扬出去，我一定以牙还牙，告诉全世界是谁吃了"千年奶酪"。

星期三

　　今天我明白了，要是我想知道罗利和那帮女生午餐时谈了啥，我只需要看他的日记就行了。我敢打赌他会把所有添油加醋的八卦事件全写下来。

　　问题是罗利的日记上锁了。就算我拿到手，我也打不开。不一会儿我计上心来。只要我买到他那种日记本，我就有钥匙。

　　于是今晚我去书店把架上最后一本日记本买下来。我只希望这是值得的。我得花掉一半的母元换钱买。我也不觉得老爸会特别乐意给我买一本"亲爱的秘密日记"。

星期四

今天体育课后，我看到罗利意外地把日记本忘在长凳上。等人都走光后，我用自己的钥匙试着打开他的日记。当然咯，我成功了。

打开后我开始看。

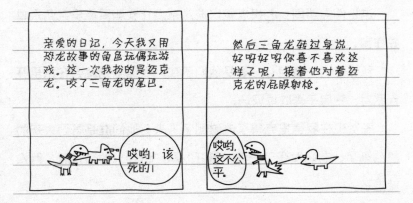

亲爱的日记，今天我又用恐龙故事的角色玩偶玩游戏。这一次我扮的是迈克龙。咬了三角龙的尾巴。

哎哟！该死的！

然后三角龙转过身说，好呀好呀你喜不喜欢这样子呢，接着他对着迈克龙的屁股射枪。

哎哟，这不公平。

我草草翻完这本日记，看里面有没有我的名字，但一页接一页全是那样的废话。

看到罗利脑袋里装些啥之后，我首先怀疑自己为什么会做了他的朋友。

星期六

这个星期以来家里诸事顺心。罗德里克得了流感，没力气骚扰我；曼尼去了奶奶家，我可以独占电视机。

昨天老爸老妈出人意料地宣布，晚上他们要出外，整个家就交托给我和罗德里克。

这是件大新闻，老妈老爸以前从来没让我和罗德里克两人单独在家。

我想他们一直担心，要是他们不在，罗德里克就会在家里开大派对，把房子弄成垃圾场。

既然现在罗德里克得了流感倒了下来，他们准是看到去玩的机会来了。老妈发表了一番"责任"和"信赖"的演讲后，两人就走了。

他们前脚刚出门，罗德里克就从沙发上一下蹦起来，直奔电话。他给他所认识的每个朋友都打电话，说他要举行派对。

我考虑过打电话给老爸老妈，向他们报告罗德里克的图谋。不过我以前从未参加过高中生的派对，所以我很好奇。我决定还是闭上嘴巴，深切体验一下高中生的派对。

罗德里克让我去地下室拿几张折叠桌上来，顺便在楼下的冰柜拿几袋冰块。晚上7:00左右罗德里克的朋友陆续出现，街上停满车子。

第一个进门的是罗德里克的朋友沃德。之后又有几个人出现，罗德里克跟我说他们需要多几张桌子。我就下楼去取了。

可我一踏入地下室，我听见在身后的门锁上了。

我把门敲得"砰砰"响，但罗德里克故意调大音响的音量，淹没我的声音。我被困了。

　　哎，我应该早就知道罗德里克会来这么一手。

　　我真是蠢，竟然以为罗德里克会让我参加他的活动。

　　听起来他们在派对上玩得很疯。我一度以为来了几个女孩，不过我不大肯定。仅透过门隙看鞋子来追踪里面的动态，太困难了。

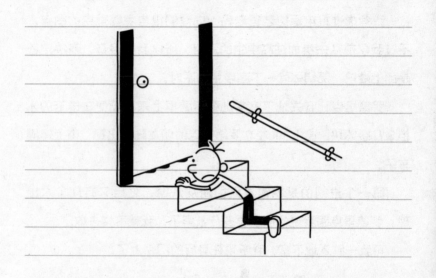

　　到了凌晨2:00，派对一点没有散场的迹象，我放弃了。这一晚余下的时间，我在地下室的空床上度过，尽管没有被子。我几乎被冻死，但我绝对不用罗德里克床上的被子。

　　我早晨醒来，门开了，一定是有人夜里打开了地下室的门。我走上楼梯一看，客厅就像遭到龙卷风袭击一样。

　　直到下午三点，罗德里克的朋友才走光。他们一走，罗德里克就跟我说要帮他清理现场。我跟他说这是痴人说梦。可罗德里克接着说，要是他东窗事发，他会把我也拖下水。

　　他说要是我不帮他收拾烂摊子，他会跟我所有朋友说我这个暑假发生的事情。

　　我简直不敢相信罗德里克会这样耍阴招。但他说得那么认真，我只好从命干活。

老妈老爸会在7:00回来，可我们现在还有成吨的活儿要干。

要除掉派对的所有痕迹真不容易，罗德里克的朋友往每个旮旯扔垃圾。搞卫生中途休息时，我想冲一碗燕麦粥喝，从盒子里掉出一个咬了一半的比萨。

到了6:45，东西差不多收拾干净了。我到楼上准备洗个澡，就在这时候我看到浴室门上写了一句话。

罗德里克
你好啊。

我用肥皂和水费了好大劲去擦，写字的家伙一定是用擦不掉的油性笔写的。

老妈老爸随时可能到家，我们死翘翘了。罗德里克灵机一动，说可以把门扉拆下，和地下室小房间的门扉掉包。

我们找来螺丝刀，马上动手。

我们最后成功卸下门栓，把门扉抬到楼下。

然后我们拆下地下室小·房间的门扉，抬上楼。

我们的时间刚刚够用。拧紧最后一颗螺丝的下一秒，老妈老爸的车停在路上了。

你可以看得出，发现自己离开后房子没塌，他们松了多大的一口气。

我觉得我们现在还没有完全过关。像老爸这样东摸摸西看看，我肯定不用多久他就会侦查出派对的事情。

好啦，这一次算罗德里克走了狗屎运，但我要说的是，他应该为曼尼不在现场而感到庆幸。曼尼是打小报告的积极分子。事实上从他会说话开始，他一直在告我的状。连我在他懂得说话之前所做的事情，他都能告发到老妈那里。

　　那时我还小，我打碎了客厅的滑动玻璃门。老爸老妈没有任何证据表明我是祸首，追究不到我身上。我完全没有受到怀疑。但我打碎玻璃的时候曼尼在场，两年之后，他出卖了我。

　　所以曼尼会说话之后，我不得不担心他说出婴儿时目睹的那些我做过的坏事。

以前我也很喜欢告状，后来我学乖了。有一次，我告发罗德里克说了一个脏字。老妈问我他说了哪个字，我就把它拼出来。那个单词真长。

　　结果是，我因为知道一个脏词怎么拼，受到了嘴巴塞肥皂的惩罚。而罗德里克逍遥法外，毫发无损。

星期一

　　明天我得交一份英语作业，要写一则"寓言"。

　　一个故事说了一件事，而它真正想说的是另一件事，这就是"寓言"。我绞尽脑汁也没找到灵感，后来我看到罗德里克在外面修他的小货车，灵感就来了。

洛里搞砸事情

作者：格雷·赫夫利

　　从前有只猴子叫洛里，尽管它老是把事情搞糟，和它一起生活的那家人仍然很爱它。

　　有一天洛里不小心摁响了门铃，每个人都以为它懂得摁门铃了。于是他们奖励了几根香蕉给它。

好吧，现在洛里走来走去，觉得自己是猴子中的天才。有一天，它听见主人说——

洛里简单的头脑马上冒出一个方案。以下是他最后想到的东西：

洛里没日没夜地工作，长话短说，最后得到的不是一辆修好的车。

这件事过后，洛里学到非常宝贵的一课：洛里是猴子，而猴子不懂修车。

 故事完啦

　　我写完之后拿给罗德里克看。我觉得他看不懂，果然我又对了。

笨蛋，猴子怎么会懂英语。

水不湿

　　我之前说过，罗德里克知道他可以用我的"秘密"对我为所欲为，所以我绝不放过每个可以占他便宜的机会。

星期三

　　今天曼尼第一天上学前班，显然这一天他过得不怎么样。

曼尼的学校其他孩子九月份就回校了。不过曼尼上星期才学会自己上厕所，所以现在他得奋起直追。

今天曼尼的学校举行万圣节派对，这可不是让曼尼认识他的新同学的好时机。

曼尼的老师只好打电话把上班的老妈叫过来，让她接曼尼回家。

我还记得我第一天上学前班的情景。我谁也不认识，战战兢兢置身于一群陌生的小孩子之中。一个叫奎因的小孩过来跟我说话。

你喜欢吃雪糕吗？

喜欢！

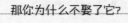

那时候我不知道这是个玩笑，被吓个半死。

我跟老妈说我不去上学前班了，还把奎因说的话告诉她。

但老妈说是奎因傻里傻气而已，不用理会他。

老妈给我解释清楚后，我觉得这个段子挺好笑的。第二天我迫不及待去上学，试用一下这个段子。

可我用这招的效果跟奎因完全不同：

致　谢

　　对于我的家人，我永远满怀感激，因为他们给我提供了我创作所需的灵感、鼓励与支持。我要好好感谢我的兄弟斯科特和帕特、我的姐姐莱，还有我的父母亲。没有你们就不会有赫夫利一家。谢谢我的太太朱莉和我的孩子们，他们为我圆梦漫画家而做出了太多牺牲。我也要谢谢我的岳父岳母，汤姆和吉儿，在我每次截稿前后他们都陪伴左右，帮前帮后。

　　感谢阿布拉姆斯出版集团的一干好汉，尤其是查理·科赫曼，一个极敬业的编辑，一个大好人，感谢我有幸与之一同亲密合作的阿布拉姆斯出版同仁：詹森·威尔斯、霍华德·李维斯、苏珊·梵·米特、查德·贝克曼、萨马拉·克莱、瓦莱里·拉尔夫和斯科特·奥尔巴赫。尤其要向米歇尔·雅各布致以谢意。

　　感谢杰斯·布莱利尔把格雷·赫夫利带向全世界。感谢贝琦·比尔德，多谢她发挥她相当的影响力来四处宣传《小·屁孩日记》。最后，感谢迪·斯科尔-弗莱，以及全国所有书商，谢谢你们把这些书送到孩子们手里。

作者简介

　　杰夫·金尼，Poptropica.com的创始人，《纽约时报》畅销榜第一畅销书《小·屁孩日记》的作者。他在华盛顿度过童年，1995

84

年移居新英格兰州。杰夫现与妻子朱莉、两个儿子威尔和格兰特居住在南马萨诸塞州。

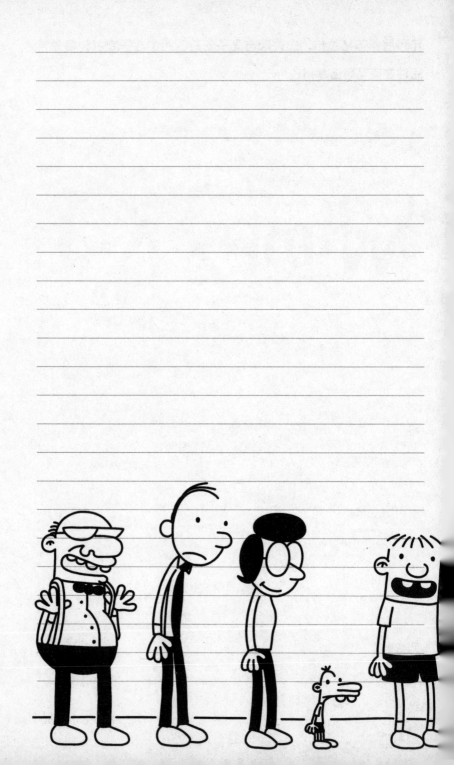

DIARY
of a
Wimpy Kid

③

by Jeff Kinney

TO JULIE, WILL, AND GRANT

SEPTEMBER

<u>Monday</u>

I guess Mom was pretty proud of herself for making me write in that journal last year, because now she went and bought me another one.

But remember how I said that if some jerk caught me carrying a book with "diary" on the cover they were gonna get the wrong idea? Well, that's exactly what happened today.

(MY BROTHER RODRICK)

Now that Rodrick knows I have another journal, I better remember to keep this one locked up. Rodrick actually got ahold of my LAST journal a few weeks back, and it was a disaster. But don't even get me started on THAT story.

Even without my Rodrick problems, my summer was pretty lousy.

Our family didn't go anywhere or do anything fun, and that's Dad's fault. Dad made me join the swim team again, and he wanted to make sure I didn't miss any meets this year.

Dad's got this idea that I'm destined to be a great swimmer or something, so that's why he makes me join the team every summer.

At my first swim meet a couple of years ago, Dad told me that when the umpire shot off the starter pistol, I was supposed to dive in and start swimming.

But what he DIDN'T tell me was that the starter gun only fired BLANKS.

So I was a whole lot more worried about where the bullet was gonna land than I was about getting myself to the other end of the pool.

Even after Dad explained the whole "starter pistol" concept to me, I was still the worst swimmer on the team.

But I did end up winning "Most Improved" at the awards banquet at the end of the summer. That's only because there was a ten-minute difference between my first race and my last one.

So I guess Dad's still waiting for me to live up to my potential.

PAT
PAT

In a lot of ways, being on the swim team was worse than being in middle school.

First of all, we had to be at the pool by 7:30 every morning, and the water was always FREEZING cold.

94

And second of all, we were all crammed into two lanes, so I always had somebody on my tail trying to get around me.

The reason we had to use two lanes was because swim practice was at the same time as the Water Jazz class.

I actually tried to convince Dad to let me do Water Jazz instead of swim team, but he wouldn't go for it.

This was the first summer the coach let us boys wear swim trunks instead of those skimpy racing trunks. But Mom said Rodrick's hand-me-down bathing suit was "perfectly fine."

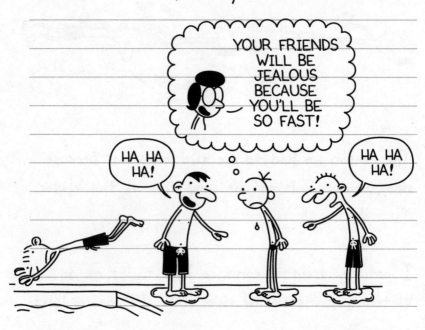

After swim practice, Rodrick would pick me up in his band's van. Mom had this crazy idea that if me and Rodrick spent "quality time" on the ride home every day, we wouldn't fight as much. But all it did was make things a lot worse.

Rodrick was always a half hour late picking me up.

And he wouldn't let me sit up front. He said the chlorine would ruin his seat, even though the van is something like fifteen years old.

Rodrick's van doesn't actually have any seats in the back, so I had to squeeze in with all the band equipment. And every time the van came to a stop, I had to pray I didn't get my head taken off by one of Rodrick's drums.

I ended up walking home every day instead of getting a ride from Rodrick. I figured it was better to just walk the two miles than to get brain damage riding in the back of that van.

Halfway through the summer, I decided I was pretty much done with swim team. So I came up with a trick to get out of practice.

I'd swim a few laps, and then I'd ask the coach if I could use the bathroom. Then I'd just hide out in the locker room until practice was over.

The only problem with my plan was that it was something like forty degrees in the boys' bathroom. So it was even colder in THERE than it was in the pool.

I had to wrap myself up in toilet paper so I didn't get hypothermia.

That's how I spent a pretty big chunk of my summer vacation. And that's why I'm actually looking forward to going back to school tomorrow.

Tuesday
When I got to school today, everybody was acting all strange around me, and at first I didn't know WHAT was up.

Then I remembered: I still had the Cheese Touch from LAST year. I got the Cheese Touch in the last week of school, and over the summer I COMPLETELY forgot about it.

The problem with the Cheese Touch is that you've got it until you can pass it on to someone else. But nobody would even get within thirty feet of me, so I knew I was gonna be stuck with the Cheese Touch for the whole school year.

Luckily, there was a new kid named Jeremy Pindle in homeroom, so that took care of THAT problem.

My first class was Pre-Algebra, and the teacher put me right next to Alex Aruda, the smartest kid in the whole class.

Alex is SUPER easy to copy off of, because he always finishes his test early and puts his paper down on the floor next to him. So if I ever get in a pinch, it's nice to know I can count on Alex to bail me out.

Kids whose last names start with the first few letters of the alphabet get called on the most by the teacher, and that's why they end up being the smartest.

Some people think that's not true, but if you want to come down to my school, I can prove it.

ALEX ARUDA   CHRISTOPHER ZIEGEL

I can only think of ONE kid who broke the last-name rule, and that's Peter Uteger. Peter was the smartest kid in the class all the way up until the fifth grade.

That's when a bunch of us started giving him a hard time about how his initials sounded when you said them out loud.

These days, Peter doesn't raise his hand at ALL, and he's pretty much a C student.

I guess I feel a little bad about the whole P.U. thing and what happened to Peter. But it's hard not to take credit whenever it comes up.

Anyway, today I got pretty decent seats in all my classes except seventh-period History. My teacher is Mr. Huff, and something tells me he had Rodrick as a student a few years back.

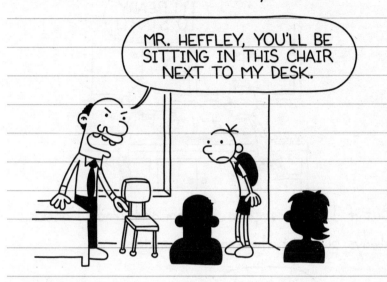

MR. HEFFLEY, YOU'LL BE SITTING IN THIS CHAIR NEXT TO MY DESK.

Wednesday

Mom has been making me and Rodrick help out more around the house, and now the two of us are responsible for doing the dishes every night.

The rule is that we're not allowed to watch any TV or play video games until all the dishes are done. But let me just say that Rodrick is the WORST dishes partner in the world.

As soon as dinner is over, he goes upstairs to the bathroom and camps out there for an hour. And by the time he comes back downstairs, I'm already done.

But if I ever complain to Mom and Dad, Rodrick always pulls out the same lame excuse:

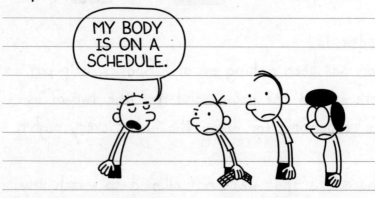

I think Mom and Dad are too worried about my little brother, Manny, to get involved in a fight between me and Rodrick right now anyway.

Yesterday, Manny drew a picture at day care, and Mom and Dad got really upset when they found it in his backpack.

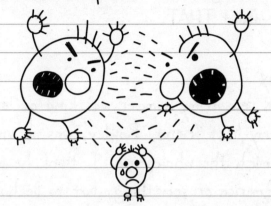

Mom and Dad thought the picture was supposed to be of THEM, so now they're acting all lovey in front of Manny.

I knew who it was REALLY supposed to be in the picture: me and Rodrick.

We got into a big blowout over the remote control the other night, and Manny was there to witness the whole thing. But Mom and Dad don't need to find out about THAT.

Thursday

Another reason my summer was kind of lame was because my best friend, Rowley, was on vacation pretty much the whole time. I think he went to South America or something, but to be honest with you, I'm not really sure.

I don't know if this makes me a bad person or whatever, but it's hard for me to get interested in other people's vacations.

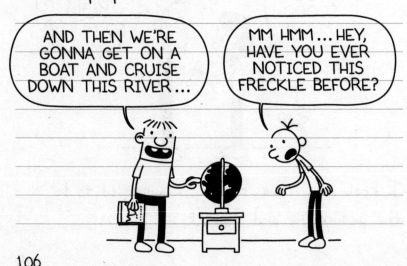

AND THEN WE'RE GONNA GET ON A BOAT AND CRUISE DOWN THIS RIVER...

MM HMM... HEY, HAVE YOU EVER NOTICED THIS FRECKLE BEFORE?

Besides, it seems like Rowley's family is always traveling to some crazy place in the world, and I can never keep their trips straight.

The other reason I don't care about Rowley's trips is because whenever Rowley comes back from one of his vacations, he always crams it down my throat.

Last year, Rowley and his family went to Australia for ten days, but from the way he acted when he got back, you'd think he lived there his whole life.

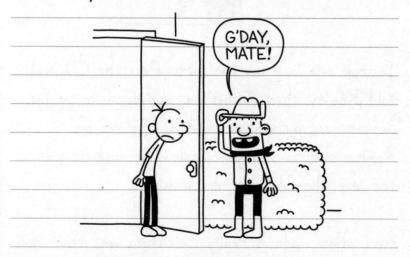

G'DAY, MATE!

Another thing that's really annoying is that whenever Rowley goes to some new country, he gets into whatever fad is going on over there.

Like when Rowley got back from Europe two years ago, he got hooked on this pop singer named "Joshie," who I guess is some huge star or something. So Rowley came back with his bags full of Joshie CDs and posters and stuff.

I took one look at the picture on the CD and told Rowley that Joshie was supposed to be for six-year-old girls, but he didn't believe me. Rowley said I was just jealous because he was the one who "discovered" Joshie.

And what made it really irritating was that now this guy was Rowley's new hero. So if I ever tried to say anything critical at all, Rowley didn't want to hear it.

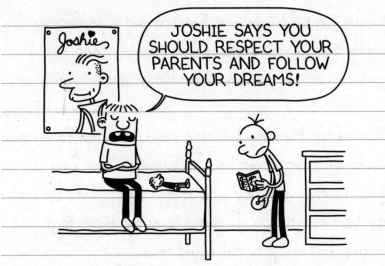

Speaking of foreign countries, today in French class, Madame Lefrere told us we're going to be choosing pen pals this year.

When Rodrick was in middle school, he had a seventeen-year-old girl from Holland as his pen pal. I know because I've seen the letters in his junk drawer.

When Madame Lefrere handed out the forms, I made sure I checked off the boxes that would get me a pen pal just like Rodrick's.

But after Madame Lefrere read over my form, she made me start over and pick again. She said I had to choose a boy who is my age, AND he has to be French. So I don't exactly have high hopes for my pen-pal experience.

Je m'appelle "Philippe."

Friday

Mom decided to start making Rodrick pick me up after school, just like he picked me up after swim practice. I guess that means she didn't learn from THAT experience. But I did. So when Rodrick picked me up today, I asked him to please take it easy on the brakes.

Rodrick said OK, but then he went out of his way to find every speed bump in town.

When I got out of the van, I called Rodrick a big jerk, and then it got physical. Mom saw the whole thing unfold from the living room window.

Mom made us come inside, and she sat us down at the kitchen table. Then she said me and Rodrick were going to have to settle our differences in a "civil manner."

Mom told me and Rodrick we each had to write down what we did wrong, and then we had to draw a picture to go along with it. And I knew exactly where Mom was going with THAT idea.

Mom used to be a preschool teacher, and whenever a kid would do something wrong, she'd make him draw a picture of it. I guess the idea was to make the kid feel ashamed of what he did so he wouldn't do it again.

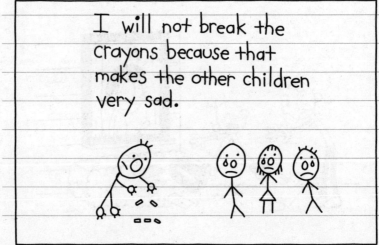

I will not break the crayons because that makes the other children very sad.

Well, Mom's idea might have worked great on a bunch of four-year-olds, but she's going to have to think of something better if she wants me and Rodrick to get along.

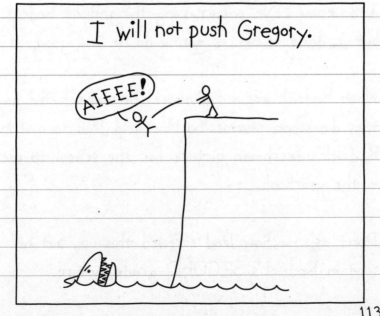

The truth is, Rodrick can pretty much treat me any way he wants, because he knows there's nothing I can do about it.

See, Rodrick is the only one who knows about this REALLY embarrassing thing that happened to me over the summer, and he's been holding it over my head ever since. So if I ever tell on him for anything, he'll spill my secret to the whole world.

I just wish I had some dirt on HIM to even things out.

I do know ONE embarrassing thing about Rodrick, but I don't think it's gonna do me any good.

When Rodrick was a sophomore, he was sick the day they did school photos. So Mom told Dad to mail in Rodrick's freshman picture for the school to use in the yearbook.

Don't ask me how Dad screwed this up, but he sent in Rodrick's SECOND-grade picture.

114

And believe it or not, it actually got printed.

| Harrington, | Hatley, | Heffley, | Hills, |
| Leonard | Andrew | Rodrick | Heather |

Unfortunately, Rodrick was smart enough to rip that page out of his yearbook. So if I'm ever gonna find something to use against him, I guess I have to keep digging.

<u>Wednesday</u>
Ever since Mom assigned the dishes to me and Rodrick, Dad's been going down to the furnace room after dinner to work on this miniature Civil War battlefield of his.

Dad spends at least three hours a night down there working on that thing. I think Dad would be happy to spend the whole weekend working on his battlefield, but Mom has OTHER plans for him.

Mom likes to rent these romantic comedies, and she makes Dad watch them with her. But I know Dad is just waiting for the first chance to break away and go back down to the basement.

Whenever Dad can't be down in the furnace room, he makes sure us kids keep away from it.

Dad won't let me or Rodrick go NEAR his battlefield, because he thinks we're gonna mess something up.

And earlier today I overheard Dad say something to Manny to make sure HE doesn't go poking around back there, either.

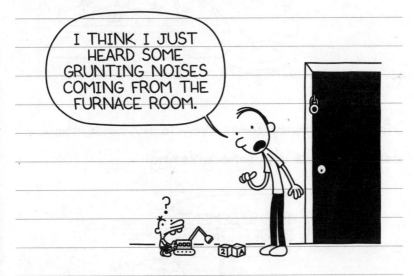

<u>Saturday</u>
Rowley came over to my house today. Dad doesn't like it when Rowley comes over, because Dad always says Rowley is "accident prone". I think it's because this one time Rowley was eating dinner here, and he dropped a plate and broke it.

So now Dad has this idea that Rowley is going to ruin his whole Civil War battlefield in one klutzy move.

Whenever Rowley comes over to my house these days, he gets the same greeting:

Rowley's dad doesn't like ME, either. That's why I don't go over to his house much anymore.

The last time I spent the night at Rowley's, we watched this movie where some kids taught themselves a secret language that no grown-ups could understand.

TRANSLATION: AT EXACTLY 2:30 P.M., LET'S ALL DROP OUR BOOKS ON THE FLOOR.

Me and Rowley thought that was pretty cool, and we tried to figure out how to talk in the same language the kids were using in the movie.

But we couldn't really get the hang of it, so we made up our OWN secret language.

Then we tried it out at dinner.

But Rowley's dad must have cracked our code, because I ended up getting sent home before dessert. And I haven't been invited to spend the night at Rowley's ever since.

When Rowley came over to my house today, he brought a bunch of pictures from his trip with him. He said the best part of his vacation was when they went on a river safari, and he showed me all these blurry pictures of birds and stuff.

Now, I've been to the Wild Kingdom amusement park a bunch of times, and they have this River Rapids ride where they have these awesome robot animals like gorillas and dinosaurs.

If you ask me, Rowley's parents should have just saved their money and taken him there instead.

DID YOU SEE ANY SHARKS FIGHTING GIANT TARANTULAS ON YOUR SAFARI?

NO. AND SHARKS DON'T FIGHT TARANTULAS.

WELL, AT WILD KINGDOM THEY DO.

But of course Rowley didn't want to hear about MY experiences, so he just gathered up his pictures and went back home.

Tonight after dinner, Mom made Dad watch one of the movies she rented, but Dad really wanted to work on his Civil War battlefield.

When Mom got up to go to the bathroom, Dad stuffed a bunch of pillows under the blanket on his side of the bed to make it look like he was asleep.

Mom didn't find out about Dad's decoy until after the movie was over.

She made Dad come to bed, even though it was only 8:30.

And now Manny sleeps in Mom and Dad's bed, because he's afraid of the monster that lives in the furnace room.

Tuesday

I thought I was done hearing about Rowley's trip, but I was wrong. Yesterday, our Social Studies teacher asked Rowley to tell the class all about his vacation, and today he came to school wearing this ridiculous costume. But what was even WORSE was when some girls came up to Rowley at lunch and started kissing his butt.

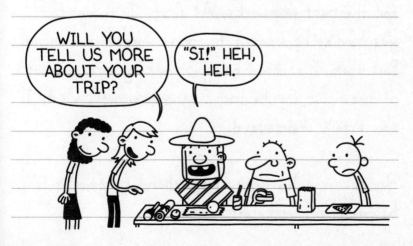

But then I realized maybe that wasn't such a
bad thing after all. So I started parading
Rowley around the cafeteria, because after all,
he IS my best friend.

Saturday
Dad has been taking me to the mall every Saturday
for the past few weeks. At first, I thought it
was because he wanted to spend more time with me.
But then I realized he's just making sure he's out
of the house for Rodrick's band practices, which I
can totally understand.

Rodrick and his heavy-metal band practice in the
basement on weekends.

The lead singer of the band is this guy named Bill Walter, and me and Dad bumped into Bill on the way out the door today.

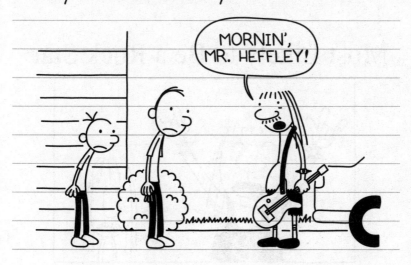

Bill doesn't have a job, and he still lives with his parents, even though he's thirty-five years old.

I'm pretty sure Dad's worst fear is that Rodrick is going to see Bill as some kind of role model, and that Rodrick will want to follow in Bill's footsteps.

So whenever Dad sees Bill, it just puts him in a bad mood for the rest of the day.

The reason Rodrick invited Bill to be in his band was because Bill got voted "Most Likely to Be a Rock Star" when HE was in high school.

Most Likely to Be a Rock Star

Bill Walter   Anna Wrentham

That hasn't really worked out for Bill yet. And I think I heard Anna Wrentham is in prison.

Anyway, me and Dad went to the mall for a few hours today, but when we got back, Rodrick's band practice wasn't over yet. You could hear the guitars and drums from a block away, and there were a bunch of random teenagers hanging out in our driveway.

I guess they must have heard the music coming out of the basement and got drawn to it, sort of like how moths get drawn to a light.

When Dad saw all those teenagers in the driveway, he TOTALLY freaked out.

Dad ran inside to call the cops, but Mom stopped him before he could dial 911.

Mom said those teenagers weren't doing any harm, and that they were just "appreciating" Rodrick's music. But I don't even know how she could say that with a straight face. And if you ever heard Rodrick's band, you'd know what I mean.

Dad couldn't relax with all those teenagers out in our driveway.

So Dad went upstairs and got his boom box. Then he put in a classical music CD and let it play. And you would not BELIEVE how quickly the driveway cleared out after that.

Dad was pretty proud of himself for thinking up that one. But Mom accused him of getting rid of Rodrick's "fans" on purpose.

Sunday

Today, on the car ride to church, I was making faces at Manny, trying to get him to laugh. I made this one face that made Manny laugh so hard that apple juice came out of his nose.

But then Mom said:

Well, once Mom put that thought in Manny's head, it was all over.

See? This is the reason I keep my distance from Manny. Every time I try to have a little fun with him, I end up regretting it.

I remember when I was younger, and Mom and Dad told me I was getting a little brother. I was REALLY excited.

After all those years of getting pushed around by Rodrick, I was definitely ready to move up a notch on the totem pole.

But Mom and Dad have always been SUPER protective of Manny, and they won't let me lay a finger on him, even if he totally deserves it.

Like the other day, I plugged in my video game system, and it wouldn't start. I opened it up and found out that Manny had stuffed a chocolate-chip cookie in the disc drive.

And of course Manny used the same excuse he ALWAYS uses when he breaks my stuff.

I really wanted to let Manny have it, but I couldn't do anything with Mom standing right there.

Mom said she would have a "talk" with Manny, and they went downstairs. A half hour later, they came back up to my room, and Manny was holding something in his hands.

It was a ball of tinfoil with a bunch of toothpicks sticking out of it.

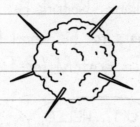

Don't ask me how that was supposed to make up for my broken video game system. I went to throw the stupid thing away, but Mom wouldn't even let me do THAT.

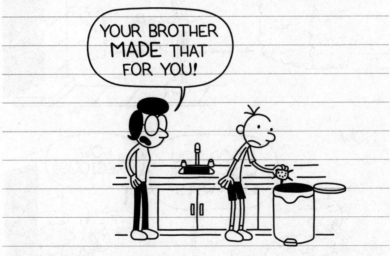

The first chance I get, that thing's going in the trash. Because mark my words, if I don't get rid of it, I'm gonna end up sitting on it.

Even though Manny drives me totally nuts, there is ONE reason I like having him around. Ever since Manny started talking, Rodrick has stopped making me sell chocolate bars for his school fund-raisers. And believe me, I'm grateful for THAT.

Madame Lefrere made us write our first pen-pal letters today. I got assigned to this kid named Mamadou Montpierre, and I guess he lives someplace in France.

I know I'm supposed to write in French and Mamadou is supposed to write in English, but to be honest with you, writing in a foreign language is pretty hard.

So I really don't see the need for both of us to stress out over this whole pen-pal thing.

Dear Mamadou,

    First of all, I think we should both just write in English to keep things simple.

By the way, remember how I said I was gonna end up sitting on Manny's spiky tinfoil ball thing? Well, I was half right.

135

Rowley came over today to play video games, and HE ended up sitting on it.

I'm actually kind of relieved, to be honest with you. I lost track of that thing a couple of days ago, and I'm just glad it finally turned up.

And in all the commotion, I threw Manny's "gift" in the garbage. But something tells me Mom wouldn't have stopped me this time.

Wednesday
Rodrick has an English paper due tomorrow, and Mom's actually making him do it himself for once. Rodrick doesn't know how to type, so he usually writes his papers out on notebook paper and then hands them off to Dad.

But when Dad reads over Rodrick's work, he finds all sorts of factual errors.

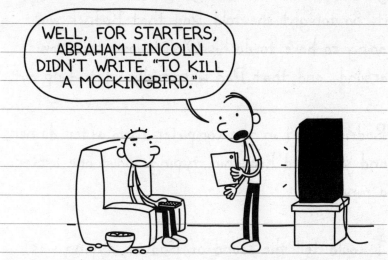

WELL, FOR STARTERS, ABRAHAM LINCOLN DIDN'T WRITE "TO KILL A MOCKINGBIRD."

Rodrick doesn't really care about the mistakes, so he tells Dad to just go ahead and type the paper like it is.

But Dad can't stand typing a paper with errors in it, so he just rewrites Rodrick's paper from scratch. And then a couple days later, Rodrick brings his graded paper home and acts like he did it himself.

This has been going on for a few years, and I guess Mom decided she's going to put an end to it. So tonight she told Dad that Rodrick was going to have to do his OWN work this time around, and that Dad wasn't allowed to help out.

Rodrick went in the computer room after dinner, and you could hear him typing about one letter a minute.

I could tell the sound of Rodrick typing was driving Dad totally bananas. On top of that, Rodrick would come out of the computer room every ten minutes and ask Dad some dumb question.

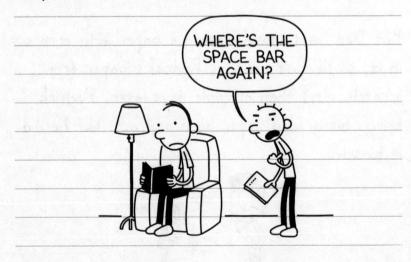

WHERE'S THE SPACE BAR AGAIN?

After a couple of hours, Dad finally cracked.

Dad waited for Mom to go to bed, and then he typed Rodrick's whole paper for him. So I guess this means Rodrick's system is safe, at least for now.

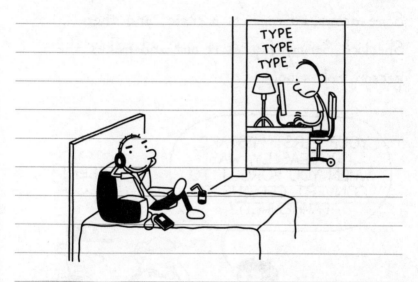

I have a book report due tomorrow, but I'm really not sweating it.

I found the secret to doing book reports a long time ago. I've been milking the same book for the past five years: "Sherlock Sammy Does It Again."

There are about twenty short stories in "Sherlock Sammy Does It Again", but I just treat each story like it's a whole book, and the teacher never notices.

These Sherlock Sammy stories are all the same. Some grown-up commits a crime, and then Sherlock Sammy figures it out and makes the person look stupid.

I'm kind of an expert at writing book reports by now. All you have to do is write exactly what the teacher wants to hear, and you're all set.

Man, Sherlock Sammy is so smart, and I'll bet that's cause he reads so many books.

I'll bet you're right!

There were a bunch of hard words in this book, but I looked them up in the dictionary so now I know what they mean.

I guess you're a bit of a "sleuth" yourself! (A+)

<u>Monday</u>

There was a kid named Chirag Gupta who was one of my friends last year, but he moved away in June. His family had a big going-away party, and the whole neighborhood came. But I guess Chirag's family must have changed their mind, because today Chirag was back in school.

Everyone was happy to see Chirag again, but a couple of us decided to have a little fun with him before officially welcoming him back.

So we basically pretended he was still gone.

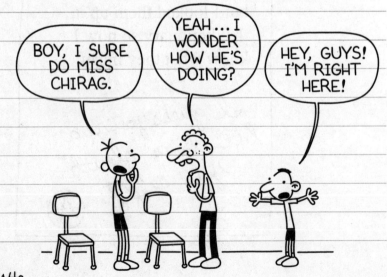

I have to admit, it was pretty funny.

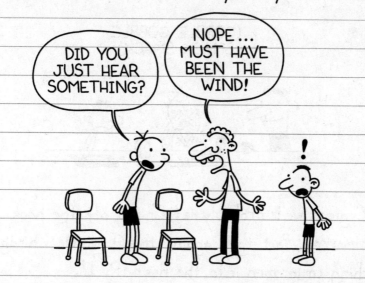

At lunch, Chirag sat next to me. I had an extra chocolate-chip cookie in my lunch bag, and I made a big deal about it.

OK, so maybe that one was a little cruel.

(GOBBLE GOBBLE
SMACK SMACK)

I guess we'll probably let Chirag off the hook tomorrow. But then again, this Invisible Chirag thing could turn into the next "P.U.".

Tuesday
OK, so the Invisible Chirag joke is still going, and the whole CLASS is in on it now. I don't want to get too far ahead of myself or anything, but I think I might have Class Clown in the bag for dreaming this one up.

In Science, the teacher asked me to count the number of kids in the classroom so she'd know how many pairs of safety goggles to get out of the closet.

144

So I made a big show of counting everyone in the room except Chirag.

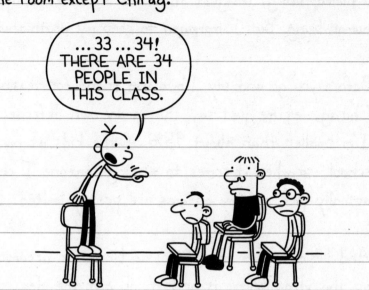

Well, that REALLY set Chirag off. He got up and started yelling, and it was really hard to stare straight ahead and act like he wasn't there.

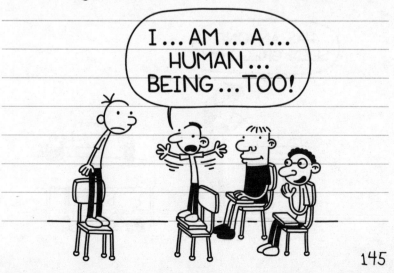

I wanted to tell him that we never said he wasn't a human being, it's just that he's an INVISIBLE human being. But I managed to keep my mouth shut.

Before you go and say I'm a bad friend for teasing Chirag, let me just say this in my own defense: I'm smaller than about 95% of the kids at my school, so when it comes to finding someone I can actually pick on, my options are pretty limited.

And besides, I'm not 100% to blame for dreaming up this idea. Believe it or not, I got the idea from Mom. This one time when I was a kid, I was playing under the kitchen table, and Mom came looking for me.

HAS ANYONE SEEN GREGORY?

I don't know what made me do it, but I decided
to play a joke on Mom and stay hidden.

Mom went all around the house calling my name.
I think she must have finally seen me under the
kitchen table, but she still pretended she didn't
know where I was.

POOR GREGORY, ALL
ALONE IN THE SNOW.
OH, BOO HOO HOO.

I thought it was pretty funny, and I probably
would've stayed hidden under there for a little
while more. But Mom finally got me to crack when
she said she was gonna give my gum-ball machine
to Rodrick.

147

So if you want to point fingers on the Invisible
Chirag joke, now you know who's really to blame.

Thursday

Well, yesterday, Chirag pretty much gave up on
trying to get anyone in our class to talk to him.
But today he found our weakness.

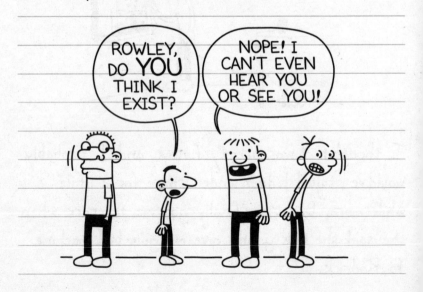

I forgot ALL about Rowley. When the joke first started up, I made sure to keep him away from Chirag, because I had a feeling Rowley would blow the joke.

But I guess I kind of got too cocky and let my guard down.

Chirag started working on Rowley at lunch, and he came really close to getting him to crack.

I could tell Rowley was about to say something, so I had to act quick. I told everyone there was a floating corn dog hovering above our lunch table, and then I plucked it out of the air and ate it in two bites.

So thanks to my quick thinking, we were able to keep the joke going.

But that REALLY made Chirag mad. He started punching my arm, but of course I had to pretend like I didn't notice.

And let me tell you, that wasn't easy to do. Chirag might be small, but that kid can really punch.

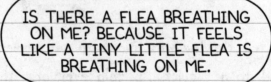

<u>Friday</u>
Well, I guess Chirag must have complained to a teacher about my little joke, because today I got called down to the front office.

When I got to Vice Principal Roy's room, he was pretty mad. He knew all about how I started the joke, and he gave me a speech about "respect" and "decency" and all that.

But luckily, Mr. Roy got one crucial fact wrong, and that was the identity of the person we were playing the joke on. So that made the apology part a whole lot easier.

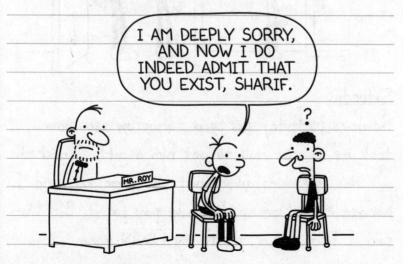

151

Mr. Roy seemed pretty satisfied with my apology, and he let me go without even tacking on any detention.

I've always heard that when Mr. Roy is done chewing a kid out, he sends them off with a pat on the back and a lollipop. And now I can tell you firsthand that it's true.

Saturday
Rowley's birthday party is tomorrow, so Mom took me to the mall to get him a gift. I picked out this cool video game that just came out, and I handed it to Mom so she could pay for it. But Mom said I had to buy it with my OWN money.

I told Mom that first of all, I have zero money.

And second of all, if I DID have any money, I wouldn't be wasting it on ROWLEY.

Mom didn't seem too happy with what I said, but it's not MY fault I'm broke. I actually had a job this summer, but the people I worked for stiffed me, so I didn't earn a single penny.

We have these neighbors named the Fullers who live a few doors up, and they go away on vacation every summer.

They usually leave their dog, Princess, in the kennel, but this year, they told me they'd pay me five bucks a day to feed Princess and take her out. I figured I'd earn enough to buy a whole pile of video games with that kind of money.

But I guess Princess is gun-shy about going to the bathroom in front of strangers, so I ended up spending a lot of time standing around in the hot sun waiting for this dumb dog to hurry up and go.

I'd wait and wait and nothing would happen, and then I'd just take Princess back inside.

But EVERY time I'd leave, Princess would make a big mess in the foyer, and I'd have to clean it up the next day. Toward the end of the summer I got smart and realized it would be a whole lot easier to just clean up all of Princess's messes at once instead of doing it every single day.

So I fed her and let her do her business on the foyer floor for about two weeks.

Then, the day before the Fullers were due back, I headed up the hill with all my cleaning supplies.

But guess what? The Fullers cut their trip short and got home a day EARLY.

I guess they didn't know it's polite to call ahead and let people know when your plans have changed.

Tonight, Mom called a house meeting with me and Rodrick. She said that the two of us are always complaining that we don't have any money, so she came up with a way for us to earn some cash.

Then she pulled out some play money she must've dug up out of a board game, and she called the money "Mom Bucks". Mom said we could earn Mom Bucks by doing chores and good deeds and stuff like that, and we could trade them in for REAL money.

Mom handed us $1,000 each to get us started. I thought I had struck it rich. But then she explained that each Mom Buck was only worth a penny of REAL money.

Mom told us how we should save up our Mom Bucks, and if we were patient, we could buy something we really wanted.

But Rodrick cashed in his whole stash before Mom was even done talking.

Then he went down to the convenience store and blew his money on some heavy-metal magazines.

If Rodrick wants to waste his money like that, he can go right ahead. But I'm gonna be smart with MY Mom Bucks.

Sunday
Today was Rowley's birthday party, and he had it at the mall. I'm sure I would have thought it was a lot of fun if I was about seven years old.

That was the average age of the kids at Rowley's party. Rowley invited his whole karate team, and most of those kids are still in elementary school. I just wish I would have known what the party was gonna be like so I could have skipped it.

We started off playing these dopey party games like Pin the Tail on the Donkey and stuff like that. The last game we played was Hide-and-Seek.

My plan was to just hide in the ball pit and stay there until the party was over. But some OTHER kid was already in there.

It turned out this kid wasn't from Rowley's party. He was from the LAST birthday party that happened an hour earlier.

I guess he must have hid in there during Hide-and-Seek, and nobody ever FOUND him.

So Rowley's party had to be put on hold while the staff tried to track down this kid's parents.

After that situation got cleared up, we had cake and watched Rowley open his gifts. He mostly got a bunch of kids' toys, but he seemed pretty happy about it.

Then Rowley's parents gave him their present.
And guess what? It was a DIARY.

It kind of ticked me off, because I knew
Rowley asked his parents for a diary so he could
be just like me. After Rowley opened his present
he said:

I let him know exactly what I thought of that
idea by slugging him in the arm. And I really
don't care that it was his birthday, either.

One thing I will say, though. I used to be mad at Mom for getting me a journal that looked too girly. But after seeing Rowley's diary, I'm not so mad anymore.

Lately, Rowley has been TOTALLY riding me. He reads the same comic books I read, drinks the same kind of soda I drink, you name it. Mom says I should be "flattered," but to be honest with you, it's totally creeping me out.

A couple days ago, I did an experiment to see just how far Rowley would go.

I rolled up one of my pant legs and tied a bandanna around my ankle and went to school that way.

Sure enough, the next day Rowley came to school wearing the same exact thing.

And that's how I ended up in Vice Principal Roy's office for the second time in a week.

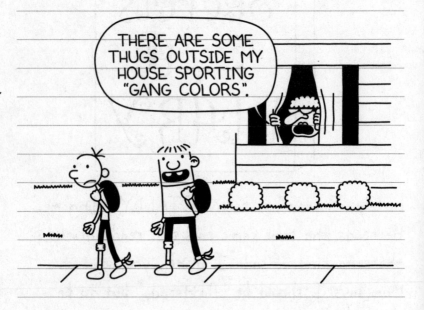

THERE ARE SOME THUGS OUTSIDE MY HOUSE SPORTING "GANG COLORS".

<u>Monday</u>
I thought I was totally in the clear for the Invisible Chirag thing. But, boy, was I wrong.

Tonight, Mom got a call from Chirag's DAD.
Mr. Gupta told Mom all about the prank we
were playing on his son, and how I was the
ringleader.

When Mom questioned me, I told her I didn't
even know what Chirag's dad was talking about.

Then Mom marched me up to Rowley's house to
hear what HE had to say.

Luckily, I was prepared for this kind of thing.
I had already drilled Rowley on what to do if
we ever got busted, and that if we both just
denied everything, we'd be OK.

But the second Mom started asking Rowley questions, he broke down.

So after our visit to Rowley's house, Mom drove me over to Chirag's to apologize. And let me tell you, THAT wasn't a whole lot of fun.

Mr. Gupta didn't seem too impressed with my apology, but believe it or not, Chirag was actually pretty cool about it.

After I apologized, Chirag invited me inside to play video games. I think he was so relieved to finally have one of his classmates talking to him again that he just decided to forgive me for the whole incident.

So I guess I forgive him, too.

Tuesday
Even though Chirag let me off the hook last night, Mom wasn't done with me yet.

She wasn't really that mad about the joke or how I treated Chirag. She was just mad that I LIED about it.

So Mom told me she'll ground me for a MONTH if she catches me lying again.

And that means I better watch my step, because Mom's not gonna forget what she said. When it comes to my screwups, Mom has a memory like an elephant.

THAT'S THE SECOND TIME YOU TRACKED MUD INTO THE KITCHEN!

(FIRST TIME: SIX YEARS AGO)

Last year Mom caught me lying, and I paid the price for it.

Mom made a gingerbread house a week before Christmas, and she put it on top of the refrigerator. She said nobody was allowed to touch it until Christmas Eve dinner.

166

But I couldn't help myself. So every night, I'd sneak downstairs and pick off a little piece of the gingerbread house. I tried to only eat a tiny piece each time so Mom wouldn't notice.

It was really hard to limit myself to one gumdrop or one little crumb of gingerbread each night, but I managed to do it anyway.

167

I didn't know how much I had actually eaten until Mom took it down off the fridge on Christmas Eve.

When Mom accused me of eating all the candy, I denied it. But I wish I just fessed up right away, because that fib totally backfired on me.

Mom had just gotten hired to write a parenting column for the local newspaper, and she was always looking for material. So that incident pretty much made me into a local celebrity.

When your child is being deceptive

Susan Heffley

The weeks leading up to Christmas can be a source of stress for a child and can harbor unforeseen temptations. My son Gregory found that

You know, now that I think about it, Mom isn't exactly squeaky clean when it comes to being honest HERSELF.

I remember when I was a kid, and she found out I wasn't brushing my teeth every night. She faked a call to the dentist's office. And that call is the reason why I still brush my teeth four times a day.

Friday
Well, it's been three days and I've kept my promise to Mom. I've been 100% honest the whole time, and believe it or not, it's not that hard.

In fact, it's kind of liberating. I've been in a
couple of situations already where I was a lot
more honest than I would have been a week ago.

For example, the other day I had a conversation
with this neighborhood kid named Shawn Snella.

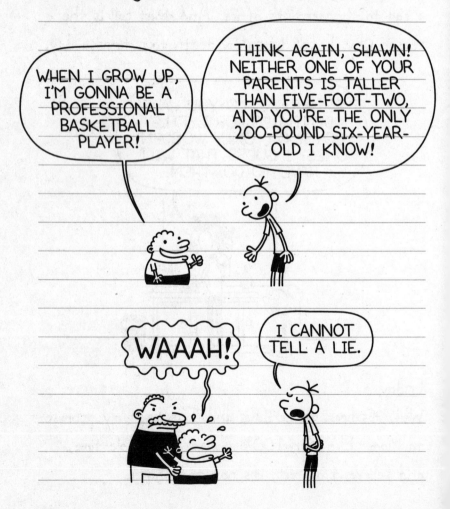

And yesterday, Rowley's family had a birthday party for his grandfather.

Most people don't seem to appreciate a person as honest as me. So don't ask me how George Washington ever got to be president.

<u>Saturday</u>
Today I answered the phone, and it was Mrs. Gillman from the PTA, looking for Mom. I tried to hand her the phone, but she whispered for me to tell Mrs. Gillman that she wasn't home.

I couldn't tell if Mom was trying to trick me into lying or WHAT, but there was no way I was going to break my honesty streak over something as dumb as THIS.

So I made Mom go out on the front porch before I said a word to Mrs. Gillman.

MY MOTHER IS NOT INSIDE THE HOUSE RIGHT NOW.

And from the look Mom gave me when she came back in the house, I kind of get the feeling she's not gonna hold me to that honesty pledge anymore.

Monday

Today was Career Day at school. They have Career Day every year to get us kids to start thinking about our future.

They brought in a bunch of adults who had all these different jobs. I think the idea is that us kids will find out about a job we like, and then we'll know what we want to be when we grow up.

But what REALLY happens is that you just find out which jobs to rule out.

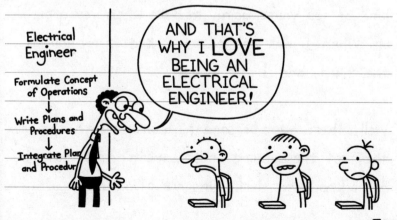

Electrical Engineer

Formulate Concept of Operations
↓
Write Plans and Procedures
↓
Integrate Plans and Procedures

AND THAT'S WHY I LOVE BEING AN ELECTRICAL ENGINEER!

After the presentations, we had to fill out these questionnaires. The first question was, "Where do you see yourself in fifteen years?"

I know EXACTLY where I'll be in fifteen years: in my pool, at my mansion, counting my money. But there weren't any check boxes for THAT option.

The questionnaires are supposed to predict what kind of job you're going to have when you grow up. When I was finished, I looked up my job on the chart, and I got "Clerk."

Well, there must be something wrong with the way they set these forms up or something, because I don't know any clerks who are billionaires.

Some other kids were unhappy with the jobs they ended up with, too. But the teacher said we shouldn't take these things too seriously.

Well, try telling that to Edward Mealey. Last year, he got "Sanitation Worker" on his job chart, and the teachers have been treating him different ever since.

Rowley got "Nurse" on his job chart, and he seemed pretty happy about it. A couple of girls got Nurse, too, and they were chatting away with Rowley after class.

Next year I have to remember to sit next to
Rowley and copy his job form so I can get in on
some of that action.

Saturday
Me and Rodrick were just sitting around the
house today, so Mom sent us over to Gramma's to
rake her leaves.

Mom said she'd pay us $100 in Mom Bucks for
each bag we filled. Plus, Gramma said she'd give us
hot chocolate after we were finished.

I really didn't feel like working on a Saturday,
but I needed the cash. Besides, Gramma makes
really awesome hot chocolate. So we got some
rakes and plastic bags from our garage and
headed down to Gramma's house.

I took one side of the yard, and Rodrick took
the other. But ten minutes into the job,
Rodrick came over and told me I was doing
everything all wrong.

Rodrick said I was putting WAY too many leaves
in each bag, and that if I just tied the bag closer
to the bottom, I could get done a lot quicker.

See, now this is the kind of advice you're SUPPOSED to get from your older brother.

After Rodrick showed me that trick, we went through bags like nobody's business. In fact, we ran out in half an hour.

Gramma didn't seem too happy about forking over the hot chocolate when we came inside. But like they say, a deal's a deal.

AHHHH!

Monday
Ever since Career Day, Rowley has been spending lunch with a bunch of girls who sit at the corner table in the cafeteria. I guess the group of them is like the Future Nurses of America or something.

Don't ask me WHAT they talk about over there. They just whisper and giggle like a bunch of first-graders.

All I can say is, they better not be talking about ME.

You remember how I said Rodrick is the only one who knows about that really embarrassing thing that happened to me over the summer? Well, Rowley knows the SECOND most embarrassing thing that ever happened to me, and I really don't need him digging it back up.

Back in fifth grade, we had a project in Spanish where we had to do a skit in front of the class, and my partner was Rowley.

We had to do the whole skit in Spanish. Rowley asked me what I would do for a candy bar, and I said I'd stand on my head.

But when I tried to do a headstand, I tipped over, and my rear end went right through the wall.

ESTARIO
PARADO
EN MI
AY-AY-AY!

Well, the school never bothered to fix the hole, so for the rest of my time in elementary school, my butt-print was on display in Mrs. Gonzales's room.

And if Rowley's spreading that story around, believe me I'm gonna tell the whole world who ate the Cheese.

<u>Wednesday</u>

Today I realized that if I wanted to know what
Rowley and those girls are talking about at lunch,
all I have to do is read his DIARY. I'll bet he's
writing down all sorts of juicy gossip in that thing.

The problem is, Rowley's diary is LOCKED. So even
if I got ahold of it, I wouldn't have any way to
open it. But then I thought of something. All I
had to do was buy the same exact diary HE has,
and then I'd have a key.

So I went to the bookstore tonight and got
the last one on the shelf. I just hope buying
this thing was worth it, because I had to cash
in half of my Mom Bucks to pay for it. And I
don't think Dad was too thrilled with the idea of
me buying a Sweet Secrets Diary, either.

Thursday

After Phys Ed today, I saw that Rowley accidentally left his diary on the bench. So when the coast was clear, I used my new key on his diary, and sure enough, it worked.

I opened it up and started reading.

> Dear Diary,
>   Today I played with my Dinoblazer action figures again. It was Mecharex vs. Triceraclops and Mecharex bited Triceraclops in the tail.
>
> OW! DARN.

And then Triceraclops
turned around and
said oh yeah well how
do you like _that_ and
he shot Mecharex right
in the heinie.

I flipped through the rest of the book to see if
my name was in there anywhere, but it was just
page after page of this garbage.

After seeing what's going on in Rowley's head,
I'm kind of starting to wonder why I'm even
friends with him in the first place.

Saturday
Things at home have been really good for about a
week. Rodrick has the flu, so he doesn't have
the energy to bother me. And Manny has been
at Gramma's, so I've had the TV all to myself.

Yesterday, Mom and Dad made a surprise announcement. They said they were going away for the night, and that me and Rodrick were in charge of the house.

That was some pretty big news, because Mom and Dad have NEVER left me and Rodrick on our own before.

I think they've always been afraid that if they go away, Rodrick is gonna have a huge party and trash the house.

But with Rodrick knocked out with the flu, they must've seen their big chance. So after Mom gave us a speech about "responsibility" and "trust" and all that, they took off.

The SECOND Mom and Dad walked out the door, Rodrick jumped up off of the couch and picked up the phone. Then he called every friend he knew and told them he was having a party.

I thought about calling Mom and Dad to tell them what Rodrick was up to, but I've never actually BEEN to a high school party before, so I was curious. I decided to just keep my mouth shut and soak it all in.

Rodrick told me to get some folding tables out of the basement and bring a couple of bags of ice out of the downstairs freezer. Rodrick's friends started to show up around 7:00, and before you knew it, there were cars parked up and down the street.

The first person to walk through the door was Rodrick's friend Ward. A bunch more people started showing up after that, and Rodrick told me we were gonna need more tables. So I went downstairs to get them.

But as soon as I stepped foot in the basement, I heard the door lock behind me.

I pounded on the door, but Rodrick just cranked up the music to drown me out. So I was stuck down there.

Man, I should've known Rodrick would go and pull something like that.

I guess it was pretty dumb of me to think
Rodrick was gonna let me in on the action.

It sounded like it was a pretty wild party. I
think some GIRLS even showed up at one
point, but I couldn't be too sure, because it was
hard to keep track of what was going on from
just looking at the bottoms of people's shoes.

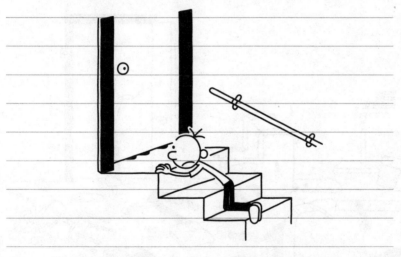

The party was still going strong at 2:00 A.M.,
but that's when I gave up. I spent the night on
one of the spare beds in the basement, even
though there were no blankets on it. I practically
froze to death, but there was no WAY I was
gonna use a blanket from Rodrick's bed.

Somebody must've unlocked the basement door overnight, because when I woke up this morning, it was open. And when I walked upstairs, it looked like a tornado had touched down in the family room.

The last of Rodrick's friends wasn't gone until 3:00 in the afternoon. And once everyone left, Rodrick told me I had to help him clean up.

I told Rodrick he was out of his mind if he thought I was helping. But then Rodrick said that if he got busted for the party, he was taking ME down with him.

He said if I didn't help him clean up the mess, he would tell all my friends about the thing that happened to me this summer.

I couldn't believe Rodrick would play dirty like that. But I could tell he was serious, so I just got to work.

Mom and Dad were supposed to be back by 7:00, and we still had a TON of work to do.

It wasn't easy to erase all the evidence of the party, because Rodrick's friends had left trash in all these crazy places. At one point, when I went to make myself a bowl of cereal, a half-eaten piece of pizza fell out of the box.

By 6:45, we had things pretty well wrapped up. I went upstairs to take a shower, and that's when I saw the message written on the inside of the bathroom door.

I tried scrubbing the writing off with soap and water, but whoever wrote that thing must've used a permanent marker.

Mom and Dad were gonna be home any minute, so I thought we were doomed. But then Rodrick had a genius idea. He said we could switch the door out and REPLACE it with a closet door from the basement.

So we got some screwdrivers and went to work.

We finally managed to get the door off its hinges, and then we carried it downstairs.

Then we got the closet door from Rodrick's room in the basement and brought it UPSTAIRS.

We made it with no time to spare. Mom and Dad's car rolled into the driveway right when we were tightening the last screw.

You could tell they were pretty relieved the house hadn't burned down while they were away.

I don't think we're totally out of the woods just yet. Because with the way Dad was poking around tonight, I'm sure it won't be long before he figures out about the party.

Well, Rodrick might have lucked out this time, but all I can say is, he should be glad MANNY wasn't there to see the party. Manny is a HUGE tattletale. In fact, he's been telling on me ever since he could talk. He's even told on me for stuff I did BEFORE he could talk.

When I was a kid, I broke the sliding glass door in the family room. Mom and Dad didn't have any evidence that I was the one who did it, so they couldn't peg it on me, and I was in the clear. But Manny was there when it happened, and two years later, he squealed on me.

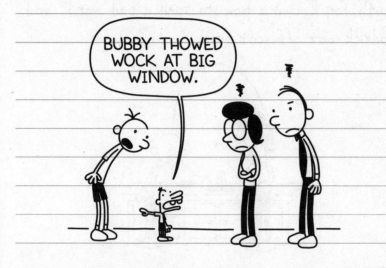

So after Manny started talking, I had to worry about all the bad things he saw me do when he was a baby.

I used to be a big tattletale myself until I learned my lesson. One time, I told on Rodrick for saying a bad word. Mom asked me which word he said, so I spelled it out. And it was a long one, too.

Well, I ended up getting a bar of soap in my mouth for knowing how to spell a bad word, and Rodrick got off scot-free.

Monday
Tomorrow, I have an English assignment due where I have to write an "allegory."

That's basically a story that says one thing but means something else. I was having trouble getting inspired, but then I saw Rodrick outside working on his van, and I got an idea.

194

Rory Screws Up
by Greg Heffley

Once upon a time there was this monkey named Rory. The family he lived with loved him very much, even though he was constantly screwing things up.

One day Rory accidentally rang the doorbell, and everybody thought he did it on purpose. So they gave him some bananas as a reward.

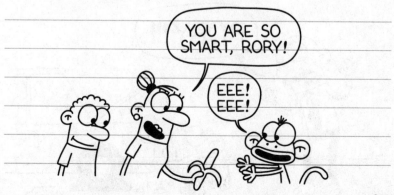

Well, now Rory was going around thinking he was some sort of monkey genius or something. And one day, he heard his owner say —

So Rory's primitive mind raced to formulate a plan. And here is what he eventually came up with:

Rory worked all day and all night, and to make a long story short, the end result was not a fixed car.

After it was all over, Rory had learned a very valuable lesson: Rory is a monkey. And monkeys don't fix cars.

THE END

After I finished my paper, I showed it to Rodrick. I figured he wouldn't get it, and sure enough, I was right.

Like I said before, Rodrick knows he's got me under his thumb with this "secret" thing. So I have to get my licks in any way I can.

<u>Wednesday</u>

Today was Manny's first day of preschool, and apparently it didn't go so great.

All the other kids in Manny's school started back in September. But Manny wasn't potty trained until last week, so that's why he had to wait until now to make the jump from day care.

Manny's preschool was having their Halloween party today, so it wasn't the greatest way to introduce him to his classmates.

Manny's teachers had to call Mom at work and have her come get him.

I remember MY first day of preschool. I didn't really know anyone, so I was pretty scared about being around a bunch of new kids. But this boy named Quinn came right over and started talking to me.

I didn't get that it was a joke, so it really freaked me out.

I told Mom I didn't want to go back to preschool, and I told her all about Quinn and what he said.

But Mom told me Quinn was just being silly, and I didn't need to listen to him.

After Mom explained the joke, I actually thought it was pretty funny. I couldn't wait to go back to school the next day and try it out myself.

But it didn't really have the same effect.

ACKNOWLEDGMENTS

I'll be forever grateful to my family for providing the inspiration, encouragement, and support I need to create these books. A huge thanks goes to my brothers, Scott and Pat; my sister, Re; and to my mom and dad. Without you, there would be no Heffleys. Thanks to my wife, Julie, and my kids, who have made so many sacrifices to make my dream of being a cartoonist come true. Thanks also to my in-laws, Tom and Gail, who have been there with a helping hand during every deadline.

Thanks to the terrific folks at Abrams, especially Charlie Kochman, an incredibly dedicated editor and a remarkable human being, and to those people at Abrams with whom I've had the pleasure of working most closely: Jason Wells, Howard Reeves, Susan Van Metre, Chad Beckerman, Samara Klein, Valerie Ralph, and Scott Auerbach. A special thanks goes to Michael Jacobs.

Thanks to Jess Brallier for bringing Greg Heffley to the world on Funbrain.com. Thanks to Betsy Bird (Fuse #8) for wielding her considerable influence to spread the word about *Diary of a Wimpy Kid*. Lastly, thanks to Dee Sockol-Frye, and to all of the booksellers across the country who put these books into kids' hands.

ABOUT THE AUTHOR

Jeff Kinney is the creator of Poptropica.com, and the author of the #1 *New York Times* bestseller *Diary of a Wimpy Kid*. He spent his childhood in the Washington, D.C. area and moved to New England in 1995. Jeff lives in southern Massachusetts with his wife, Julie, and their two sons, Will and Grant.

望子快乐

朱子庆

　　在一个人的一生中，"与有荣焉"的机会或有，但肯定不多。因为儿子译了一部畅销书，而老爸被邀涂鸦几句，像这样的与荣，我想，即使放眼天下，也没有几人领得吧。

　　儿子接活儿翻译《小屁孩日记》时，还在读着大三。这是安安第一次领译书稿，多少有点紧张和兴奋吧，起初他每译几段，便飞鸽传书，不一会儿人也跟过来，在我面前"项庄舞剑"地问："有意思么？有意思么？"怎么当时我就没有作乐不可支状呢？于今想来，我竟很有些后悔。对于一个喂饱段子与小品的中国人，若说还有什么洋幽默能令我们"绝倒"，难！不过，当安安译成杀青之时，图文并茂，我得以从头到尾再读一遍，我得说，这部书岂止有意思呢，读了它使我有一种冲动，假如时间可以倒流，我很想尝试重新做一回父亲！我不免窃想，安安在译它的时候，不知会怎样腹诽我这个老爸呢！

　　我宁愿儿子是书里那个小屁孩！

　　你可能会说，你别是在做秀吧，小屁孩格雷将来能出息成个什么样子，实在还很难说……这个质疑，典型地出诸一个中国人之口，出之于为父母的中国人之口。望子成龙，一定要孩子出息成个什么样子，虽说初衷也是为了孩子，但最终却是苦了孩子。"生年不满百，常怀千岁忧。"现在，由于这深重的忧患，我们已经把成功学启示的模式都做到胎教了！而望子快乐，有谁想过？从小就快乐，快乐一生？惭愧，我也是看了《小屁孩日记》才想到这点，然而儿子已不再年少！我觉得很有些对不住儿子！

我从来没有对安安的"少年老成"感到过有什么不妥，毕竟少年老成使人放心。而今读其译作而被触动，此心才为之不安起来。我在想，比起美国的小屁孩格雷和他的同学们，我们中国的小屁孩们是不是活得不很小屁孩？是不是普遍地过于负重、乏乐和少年老成？而当他们将来长大，娶妻（嫁夫）生子（女），为人父母，会不会还要循此逻辑再造下一代？想想安安少年时，起早贪黑地读书、写作业，小四眼，十足一个书呆子，类似格雷那样的调皮、贪玩、小有恶搞、缰绳牢笼不住地敢于尝试和行动主义……太缺少了。印象中，安安最突出的一次，也就是读小学三年级时，做了一回带头大哥，拔了校园里所有单车的气门芯并四处派发，仅此而已吧（此处，请在家长指导下阅读）。

说点别的吧。中国作家写的儿童文学作品，很少能引发成年读者的阅读兴趣。安徒生童话之所以风靡天下，在于它征服了成年读者。在我看来，《小屁孩日记》也属于成人少年兼宜的读物，可以父子同修！谁没有年少轻狂？谁没有豆蔻年华？只不过呢，对于为父母者，阅读它，会使你由会心一笑而再笑，继以感慨系之，进而不免有所自省，对照和检讨一下自己和孩子的关系，以及在某些类似事情的处理上，自己是否欠妥？等等。它虽系成人所作，书中对孩子心性的把握，却准确传神；虽非心理学著作，对了解孩子的心理和行为，也不无参悟和启示。品学兼优和顽劣不学的孩子毕竟是少数，小屁孩格雷是"中间人物"的一个玲珑典型，着实招人怜爱——在格雷身上，有着我们彼此都难免有的各样小心思、小算计、小毛病，就好像阿Q，读来透着与我们有那么一种割不断的血缘关系，这，也许就是此书在美国乃至全球都特别畅销的原因吧！

　　最后我想申明的是，第一读者身份在我是弥足珍惜的，因为，宝贝儿子出生时，第一眼看见他的是医生，老爸都摊不上第一读者呢！

我眼中的😛……

★ 我女儿买回家当天就一口气读了六十多页。第二天晚上睡觉前我跟她说："妈妈今晚有事，你自己读会书就睡觉吧。"结果到了凌晨一点钟发现她屋里的灯还亮着！还在读！简直咣当一声晕倒在地。赶紧关灯逼她睡觉。第二天我一看，两百多页的书她已读到一百八十多页。

——Amour

★ 俺家老二是个不喜欢读书的孩子，记忆中好像只有这本书是一口气看下来的，他的几个朋友都很喜欢，大家传来传去还限定时间看完，因为老有人等着。这本书是卡通式的，书中的卡通图和字都是出于作者的铅笔之下。那些画，非常CUTE！这本书简直太棒了。尤其适合那些读过初中或着想笑得发狂的人来读。

——Anaya

★ 打破正襟危坐的学英文心魔，让长者或孩子都可以在如偷窥般的阅读形式下，轻松读懂美国"囧男孩"的芝麻心事，然后你发现：不知不觉间，竟然多会好多英文单词和用语！放下书，一起开始写英文日记吧！

——作家、作词家、主持人陈乐融

★ 格雷的麻烦事和恶作剧实在是太好笑了。我简直等不及想看到本书改编的电影了！

——Adam

★ 有趣！酷！绝对是我读过的最有意思的一本书！

——Alanna

★ 我非常喜欢这本书，我已经读了三遍了。要想在中学里"混"下去，这绝对是本不可不读的书。

——Diego

★ 如果你喜欢看漫画或是喜欢读别人的日记，那就一定会喜欢这本书，我100%地保证。

——Alexa

★ 嘿嘿，我只用了不到一天时间就一口气把整本书读完了。

——Andrew

★ 我要向所有想大笑的人推荐这本书。这是我喜欢的一本书，因为它可不像其他那些书那样，整篇整篇全是文字，看得你头昏脑涨。读这本书时，我简直是一路笑个不停，旁边的人还以为我出了毛病……

——ZOOM Fan

　　亲爱的读者，你看完这本书后，有什么感想吗？请来电话或是登陆本书的博客与我们分享吧！等本书再版时，这里也许换上了你的读后感呢！

　　我们的电话号码是020－83795744，博客地址是：blog.sina.com.cn/wimpykid。

悦读"小·屁孩"

美国超级畅销书《小屁孩日记》系列，迄今已连续100周蝉联《纽约时报》童书套书排行榜榜首，全美畅销超过3000,000册！简体中文版由新世纪出版社独家出版发行！正在热销……每册仅售14.9元！

《小·屁孩日记①——鬼屋创意》

在日记里，格雷记叙了他如何驾驭充满冒险的中学生活，如何巧妙逃脱学校歌唱比赛，最重要的是如何不让任何人发现他的秘密。他经常想捉弄人反被人捉弄；他常常想做好事却弄巧成拙；他屡屡身陷尴尬境遇竟逢"凶"化吉。他不是好孩子，也不是坏孩子，就只是普通的孩子；他有点自私，但重要关头也会挺身而出保护朋友……

《小·屁孩日记②——谁动了千年奶酪》

在《小屁孩日记②》里，主人公格雷度过一个没有任何奇迹发生的圣诞节。为打发漫长无聊的下雪天，他和死党罗利雄心勃勃地想要堆出"世界上最大的雪人"，却因为惹怒老爸，雪人被销毁；格雷可是不甘寂寞的，没几天，他又找到乐子了，在送幼儿园小朋友过街的时候，他制造

一起"虫子事件"吓唬小朋友，并嫁祸罗利，从而导致一场"严重"的友情危机……格雷能顺利化解危机，重新赢得好朋友罗利的信任吗？

《小·屁孩日记③——好孩子不撒谎》

在本册里，格雷开始了他的暑假生活。慢着，别以为他的假期会轻松愉快。其实他整个暑假都被游泳训练班给毁了。他还自作聪明地导演了一出把同学齐拉格当成隐形人的闹剧，他以为神不知鬼不觉就可以每天偷吃姜饼，终于在圣诞前夜东窗事发，付出了巨大的代价……

《小·屁孩日记④——偷鸡不成蚀把米》

本集里，格雷仿佛落入了他哥哥罗德里克的魔掌中一般，怎么也逃脱不了厄运：他在老妈的威逼利诱下跟罗德里克学爵士鼓，却只能在一旁干看罗德里克自娱自乐；与好友罗利一起偷看罗德里克窝藏的鬼片，却不幸玩过火害罗利受伤，为此格雷不得不付出惨重代价——代替罗利在全

校晚会上表演魔术——而他的全部表演内容就是为一个一年级小朋友递魔术道具。更大的悲剧还在后面，他不惜花"重金"购买罗德里克的旧作业想要蒙混过关，却不幸买到一份不及格的作业。最后，他暑假误入女厕所的囧事还被罗德里克在全校大肆宣扬……格雷还有脸在学校混吗？他的日记还能继续下去吗？